Carol Marinelli recently filled in a form asking for her job title. Thrilled to be able to put down her answer, she put 'writer'. Then it asked what Carol did for relaxation and she put down the truth—'writing'. The third question asked for her hobbies. Well, not wanting to look obsessed, she crossed her fingers and answered 'swimming'—but, given that the chlorine in the pool does terrible things to her highlights, I'm sure you can guess the real answer!

Books by Carol Marinelli

Mills & Boon Medical Romance

Desert Prince Docs
Seduced by the Sheikh Surgeon

The Hollywood Hills Clinic
Seduced by the Heart Surgeon

Baby Twins to Bind Them
Just One Night?
The Baby of Their Dreams
The Socialite's Secret

Mills & Boon Modern Romance

The Billionaire's Legacy
Di Sione's Innocent Conquest

The Sheikh's Baby Scandal

Visit the Author Profile page at
millsandboon.co.uk for more titles.

She wanted a kiss, Daniel knew, but he was also certain that she wanted a whole lot more than that. Not just sex, but the part of himself he refused to give.

'What?' he said again, and then his face broke into a smile as, very unexpectedly, Holly— sweet Holly—showed another side of herself.

'Are you going to make me invite you in?'

'Yes.'

'You're not even going to try and persuade me with a kiss?' Holly checked.

'You want me or you don't.' Daniel shrugged. 'There's no question that I want you. But Holly, do you get that—?'

She knew what was coming and she didn't need the warning. He had made his position perfectly clear so she interrupted him. 'I don't need the speech.'

She just needed this.

Dear Reader,

I hope you enjoy reading about Daniel and Holly as much I did writing about them.

For me, Christmas is such a special time, and I enjoy every moment of the build-up and all the tradition that surrounds it. I know, though, that Christmas can be a difficult time for a lot of people. My hero, Daniel, just wants Christmas to be over and done with, and he has no interest in all the festivities. Certainly the last thing he wants is romance. I love writing *opposites attract* stories, and my heroine, Holly, not only adores Christmas, she is head-over-heels in love with Daniel too!

This is my first story set in The Primary Hospital in London—a busy, modern teaching hospital—and I am looking forward to writing many more.

Happy reading,

Carol x

PLAYBOY ON HER CHRISTMAS LIST

BY
CAROL MARINELLI

Published in Great Britain 2016
By Mills & Boon, an imprint of HarperCollins*Publishers*
1 London Bridge Street, London, SE1 9GF

© 2016 Carol Marinelli

ISBN: 978-0-263-06593-0

Printed and bound in Great Britain
by CPI Antony Rowe, Chippenham, Wiltshire

CHAPTER ONE

'HOLLY, PUT THE decorations back. I've already told you that there are quite enough already. This is the emergency department, *not* the children's ward.'

Holly, dressed in baggy scrubs and weighted down with tinsel and glittery silver snowmen, jumped when she heard Kay's strong Irish accent and realised that the nurse unit manager was sitting at the nurses' station.

Caught!

Holly had also thought that locum registrar Daniel Chandler was on his supper break but, no, he was drinking a coffee at the desk. Holly's blush spread like spilled red wine across her chest as she stood, dripping glitter, and was scolded in front of the very suave Daniel.

'I thought that you'd gone home,' Holly admitted to Kay.

'I know that you did,' Kay tartly responded, but then she let out a long sigh. 'I'm staying back to try and sort out the Christmas roster.'

'But it's already done.' Holly frowned. The last thing she wanted were any alterations to the roster—her plans to be with her family over the festive break had been made weeks ago. But Kay had other ideas and proceeded to tell Holly the reasons that things might have to change.

'Yes, but since then I've had two members of staff go

on extended sick leave. Thank goodness for Nora, she's offered to work Christmas night but things are *very* tight. Now, put the tinsel back where it belongs, please and, when you've done that, tie up your hair.'

'It's already tied up.'

'No, Holly, it's not.'

Holly's long, curly brown hair always started the shift in a neat ponytail and then proceeded to work its way out of its confines, curl by wild curl.

As Holly slunk back to the storeroom Daniel found himself smiling.

He'd only been doing locum shifts at The Primary for a couple of months but it was enough to know that Holly Jacobs took her Christmas decorations very seriously. She had been waiting all afternoon for Kay, who was supposed to have finished at four, to go home so that Holly could, as she put it, 'Christmas the place up'.

The Primary Hospital was a modern, busy, North London teaching hospital. It was very different in character from the prestigious Royal, where Daniel had started as a medical student and worked his way up to Accident and Emergency Registrar.

Working at The Primary was a step down, his father, an esteemed professor of surgery, would say. Certainly, renowned Professor Marcus Chandler could never fathom why his son was doing locum shifts at various hospitals around London when he could have any hours he chose at the Royal.

For Daniel, though, working at The Primary felt, if not a step up, then a step in the right direction. When he had commenced his first shift here Kay had rolled her eyes at the prospect of giving a tour to yet another temporary doctor but had soon realised Daniel was very good at his job.

More importantly, Daniel was really enjoying his work. Here there was no reputation to uphold; instead, he was slowly making his own.

And it had been noticed.

'You know there's a consultant's position coming up,' Kay said. She stared at the computer as she spoke.

'I do,' Daniel responded, and confirmed that he had been approached. 'I've already told Mr Edwards that I'm not interested.'

'Are we not good enough for you, Daniel?'

'There was a consultant's position at the Royal when I left,' Daniel pointed out. 'I wasn't interested then either.'

'You're a mystery,' Kay said, and gave a soft laugh then brushed from the desk some glitter dust that Holly had left in her wake. 'Holly would have glitter everywhere,' she tutted. 'It's an emergency department, not Santa's Grotto. People don't need festivities waved in their face when they come here. This time of year is often hard enough for our patients. I'm already over Christmas and it's only the second of December.'

'You're preaching to the converted,' Daniel agreed.

'Are you not a fan of Christmas?' Kay asked.

'Nope.'

'Nor me,' Kay agreed. 'It brings out the worst in everyone. You should see this place on Christmas night.' She got back to the staring at the computer screen, though she carried on chatting with Daniel. 'Are you going to the emergency department Christmas party tonight?'

'Nope.'

Kay laughed at his truculent response but then she frowned. 'How come you're still here? I thought you were just doing a few locums until your friend got married. The wedding was last week, wasn't it?'

'It was.' Daniel nodded and carried on writing.

He had finished up his role at the Royal at the end of September and had just been killing time until his best friend Rupert's wedding had taken place. Soon he would be taking a year off. First he would hit the ski slopes in Switzerland and then…well, he'd see what happened when it happened.

'Why didn't you just start your travels and fly back for the wedding?' Kay asked.

'Oh, no…' Daniel shook his head. 'Once I'm gone, I'm gone for good.'

'That sounds profound!' Holly was back, minus tinsel and snowmen. Her hair had been scraped back into an even tighter ponytail but was now dotted with glitter. She had a worried expression aimed at Kay because she really *needed* Christmas off this year.

Holly knew that, if the roster had to be changed, she didn't really have a leg to stand on—around this time last year her mother had been diagnosed with breast cancer. Then, despite Holly being rostered to work Christmas and New Year, Kay had been wonderful, giving Holly ten days off so that she could have some family time.

The trouble was, a cancer diagnosis didn't follow a specified timeline with a neat conclusion to signal the end.

The last year had been a fraught one, with Holly taking her little red car up and down the motorway every chance she could and wrestling the off duty around her mother's treatment. Esther had recently had to have a second round of chemotherapy, and while the news was a whole lot better Esther really wanted her family home for Christmas.

And lately, what Esther wanted, Esther got!

Holly blew out a tense breath. She loved her family dearly but things had been a bit difficult lately, to say the least.

While she hoped that Kay would understand when she came to make the necessary changes Holly needed to be sure. 'Kay, could I have a word?'

'If it's about the Christmas roster, the answer is no. Your request has been noted. And, yes,' she added. 'I do know it's also your birthday.'

'Were you a Christmas baby, Holly?' Daniel asked.

'Why do you think I'm called Holly?'

'Because you're so prickly.'

It was a small joke—Holly was the *least* prickly person. She was happy and sunny and that they could tease each other about such things without having to explain they were joking, well, it was sort of where they were at.

'So,' Daniel asked, 'do you miss out on your birthday?'

'No.' Holly shook her head. 'My parents always make sure that both are celebrated.'

'Of course they do, Polly.'

She got the Pollyanna insinuation and gave him a sweet smile. 'Better than cynical. So,' she asked, returning to the conversation she had walked in on the tail end of, 'why didn't you just fly home for the wedding?'

'There was the stag night to organise,' Daniel explained. 'Actually, there were two of them.'

'You could have just flown back for a couple of weeks.' Holly repeated Kay's assumption but Daniel shook his head.

'Rupert had a highly strung bride-to-be who was worried that I'd be a no-show if I left the country. She was actually right to be concerned—as I said, when I'm gone, I'm gone.'

Holly didn't like that.

Daniel had worked quite a few shifts now and she was getting used to having him around.

Or rather she was starting to get used to the feeling that an egg beater had been set at full whisk in the middle of her chest.

Daniel was, for want of a better word, gorgeous.

Yes, yes, he was tall and had thick black hair and a scent that had her toes curl, he had *all* of that but it was his eyes that had first sent Holly's world spinning.

Absolute navy.

It was as if the artist had meant to get back and add silvery flecks and little dots of aqua but had forgotten to. Yet he was no unfinished masterpiece. Those eyes were just this delicious navy rimmed with a halo of black and, at first look, Holly had been unable to stop staring. She had wanted to apologise, to explain she was looking for said silver specks and dots of aqua, but instead she had stared.

And so had he.

At green eyes that had appeared startled.

'Is everything okay?' he had checked.

'I have an abdo pain…' Holly had attempted to explain that she had a patient she would like him to see in Cubicle Four but she had been so flustered that it had come out all wrong. 'And vomiting.'

'Then go and lie down and let me take a look at you.'

His voice was snobby, his humour *hers,* and she had been tempted, almost, to call his bluff and do just that. Instead she had smiled. 'I'll see you in Cubicle Four.'

Holly's abdo pain had turned out to be a twenty-year-old with query appendicitis. Daniel had walked in to where Holly had been holding a bowl for the patient and he had given her a tiny smile to insinuate he had rather hoped she had been lying in wait for him.

'Pity,' he'd said.

Yet a little flirt, though huge to Holly, was just a walk in the park for him. He was suave and from what she gathered he dated a lot, and, in truth, neither was the other's type.

Except...

'What was the wedding like?' Holly asked. She was curious to know more about the reason for delaying his trip.

'Like all weddings are,' Daniel said, as Holly jumped up and sat on the bench beside where he was trying to write his notes. 'Long.'

'What did the bride wear?' she asked.

'From memory, a dress,' Daniel said. 'Possibly it was white.'

'I love winter weddings,' Holly sighed. 'Especially if it's snowing.'

'The church was freezing,' Daniel told her, and from his voice it was clear that he had a rather less dreamy take on things. 'And then it poured with rain for the photos.'

'Who was your plus one?' Kay asked, without turning her head from the computer screen.

'I never take a plus one to a wedding.' Daniel shook his head. 'Well, I haven't for a long time. I learnt the hard way that if you bring a date she assumes that it must mean you're serious. Anyway, I was the best man for this one so all that was expected from me in that department was to get off with the chief bridesmaid.'

'And did you?' Kay asked.

'That would be telling,' Daniel said. 'And I never do.'

He looked at Holly then—just an itsy-bitsy look that told her she'd be in very discreet hands.

God, he was forward!

Yet she smiled at the tiny flirt behind Kay's back.

'Anyway,' Daniel continued, 'I wanted to do the right thing by Rupert. He was very good to me when...' He didn't finish, or rather he just didn't continue with what he had started to say. 'He's a very good friend.'

'So how come you weren't out on the first flight after the wedding?' Kay pushed.

'Just...' He gave a small shrug and it was there that the conversation ended.

Daniel simply didn't answer—he did that a lot.

He might be forward with his flirting but when a conversation veered too close to personal he simply halted it.

Daniel got back to his notes and, interlude over, Kay carried on staring at the off duty, but finally she gave in.

'I'm going home,' Kay said, and closed up the screen. 'Daniel, shall we see you again?'

'I don't think so,' he answered.

Locums came and locums went but Kay gave him a smile that told Daniel he would be missed. 'Well, safe travels,' she said, and then turned to Holly. 'I'll see you tonight at the pub. The night staff should be coming in a little bit early so that the late staff can get to the party at a reasonable time. How are you getting there?'

'Taxi,' Holly said. 'Anna, Laura and I are sharing. Do you want to come with us, Daniel? There's room for one more.'

'I'm not going.'

He offered no reason and thankfully he didn't look up as he spoke because, despite her best efforts, Holly knew her shoulders had briefly slumped, but quickly she righted herself.

Actually, it was good news that he wasn't coming tonight.

The way Holly felt she was at high risk of doing something very stupid where Daniel Chandler was concerned.

Stupid as well as pointless, given that this was his last shift and that very soon he'd be heading off overseas.

Daniel, she had heard, was very into casual one-night stands. Whereas she was the complete opposite.

With one possible exception.

Him.

Oh, it would be bliss to be bad.

Sometimes, all joking and flirting aside, she felt him looking at her and there was a tension between them that Holly was almost convinced wasn't one-sided. Of course, Daniel was a natural-born flirt, but it wasn't just that, there was something in his eyes that could flip her stomach like a pancake...

Egg analogy again, Holly thought to herself, and decided that she must be hungry.

'I'm going to go for my supper break while it's quiet. I'll see you later, Kay.'

'You shall,' Kay said. 'Oh, wait. I got you a present.' She smiled at Daniel. 'I got you one too.'

Kay was big on presents.

Silly things, happy things, she passed on what had made her smile. Her charity wasn't just for the staff, though—there were regular fundraisers held throughout the year on behalf of the homeless.

Kay took the displaced seriously.

She took an overfull bag from beneath the bench and handed them both a slim card from a choice of many.

'An Advent calendar!' Holly beamed.

'I got them at the discount store,' Kay said, clearly delighted with her purchase. 'There's one for everyone.'

'There's chocolate in here,' Daniel said, opening up one of the little windows.

'Of course there is. Have you never had an Advent calendar?' Kay checked.

'Actually, no.'

'It's December the second so you get to eat two,' she told him, 'but after that it's just one a day.'

Daniel gave Holly a sideways smile that told her all twenty-five would be eaten the very moment Kay had gone and Holly smiled back as she shook her head. 'One a day,' she warned him.

'I'm lousy at self-restraint.'

Ouch.

Sometimes, in fact a little too often, he threw out those lines and usually Holly could shrug them off, but it had been getting harder and harder to of late.

'Well, I've got excellent self-control,' Holly replied, and watched the slight questioning rise of one eyebrow.

They were talking about chocolate, Holly told herself.

At least where chocolate was concerned she had self-control.

Where Daniel was concerned it was melting just as fast. It was a good job that he was leaving, Holly decided.

She had a king-size crush on him and she wasn't used to them, well, not for a very long time. At twenty-eight, Holly had rather thought that the days of wild dreams and fixating on someone's every word were long since gone.

They weren't.

Kay was just about to go when Laura, the nurse in charge this evening, came in swiftly.

'Holly—Resus,' she said. 'We've got a cardiac arrest coming in. Fifty-five-year-old male collapsed at home.'

Holly nodded and, supper forgotten, she jumped down from the bench and Daniel got down from his stool to go and prepare for the incoming patient.

'I'll just stay and see if I'm needed...' Kay offered. And Holly was expecting Laura to, as she usually did, point out that they'd be fine and could more than cope but instead Laura gave Kay a worried look.

'Can I have a quick word, Kay?' she asked.

As Laura pulled Kay aside Holly put out an arrest call to alert the medical team to come to Emergency and then started to set up for the incoming patient. Until the team arrived Daniel would be in charge but from working with him she knew that he could more than cope with anything that presented.

'What's going on?' Daniel asked, as he taped some syringes to the vial of medication he'd just pulled up in anticipation of the patient's arrival. He nodded in the direction of Laura and Kay, who were still huddled together and talking.

'I'm not sure.' Holly frowned. 'But something is.'

The alert meant that they had everything ready for the patient, going on the information they had, but just as a blue light flashed in the high windows above, Kay came over and offered more.

'Holly,' Kay said, and her voice was serious as she pulled on a plastic apron to indicate she would be participating in the resuscitation. 'The patient is Nora's husband.'

Holly swallowed. Nora Hewitt was second in charge to Kay and everyone adored her. More importantly, Paul, Nora's husband, was the good man behind a great woman. He was often at the department, picking up Nora or bringing in the lunch she had forgotten and had left sitting in the fridge at home. He always had a friendly word for everyone and should have been at the emergency department Christmas party tonight with his wife.

Instead, he was being raced into Resus on the very edge of death.

There were the sounds of sobs and tears coming from outside, though Holly could tell that it wasn't Nora.

'The daughter is *very* upset,' the paramedic informed them.

'Anna—' Kay called for assistance '—can you stay with the family?'

'Where's the team?' Holly asked in an urgent tone, desperate for them to appear so that Paul could be given the very best chance.

'We'll be fine,' Daniel said in his composed deep voice and Holly glanced over at him.

He was at the head of the resuscitation bed that the paramedics were moving Paul onto and Daniel was his usual mixture of aloof and calm.

It was everything that was needed now.

CHAPTER TWO

'ON MY COUNT,' Daniel said, and Paul was transferred from the ambulance stretcher onto the solid resuscitation bed.

Everyone was a touch flustered. All the staff knew Nora, including the paramedics, and so this was incredibly personal.

But not to Daniel.

He checked the placement of the breathing tube and looked at the monitor once Paul had been transferred to the emergency department equipment. He asked Kay to recommence massage and called for the necessary drugs and did all this as he listened to the handover.

Apparently things had been rather chaotic back at the house. Paul's daughter and her boyfriend had become agitated and distressed and had got somewhat in the way.

'He was in the bathroom when he collapsed.'

'Was someone with him?'

'It was hard to get a clear history.'

Daniel nodded as Holly handed him the drug he had asked for but, aware that everyone was tense and there was the potential for mistakes to be made, he checked and double-checked everything.

Paul was still in an arrhythmia and not responding to drugs, and though he had been shocked several times both at home and en route they had been unable to revert him to a normal rhythm. Daniel delivered more of the same and then called for the defibrillator to be charged and asked for fresh pads to be placed on Paul's chest.

Holly could see that her hands were shaking as she did as asked.

'Is anybody getting a fuller history from the family?' Daniel checked.

'I've sent Anna in to speak with Nora,' Kay said. 'I don't think he has any previous history, though.'

'I want to hear what Nora says.' Daniel was firm. This was no time for hearsay and Kay nodded as for now they worked on.

The emergency team started to arrive and gradually took over. Daniel had it all under control so that they were able to get a full handover as he worked on. Kay was massaging Paul's chest and her face was red and sweating.

'Can you take over, Holly?' she asked.

Holly did so. She was slight and really had to put in an effort to deliver effective massage. She glanced up at the clock and then back to Paul. There had been absolutely no response since he had collapsed back at home.

'Step back,' Mr Dawson, the cardiologist, ordered, and Holly climbed from the bed and once she was safely standing back another shock was delivered.

'So he collapsed at five?' Mr Dawson checked the timeline of events.

It was now five forty-five...

Holly could smell burning from the repeated shocks to his body and she looked over at Kay, who looked up at the clock.

'Was he found collapsed?' Mr Dawson checked.

'We're just waiting to have that verified,' Daniel said. The paramedics had been very thorough in their treatment and had done well but there were still some gaps in the history.

Anna came in then. 'There's no previous history and he's on no medication. Paul was standing in the bathroom, chatting to Nora, when he developed chest pain. Nora sat him on the floor and called for an ambulance. She gave him some aspirin and stayed with him, and a couple of moments later he arrested and she commenced resuscitation straight away.'

It had been a witnessed arrest, which was incredibly relevant, especially given Nora's skills. It was now evident that he'd had effective cardiac massage delivered from the very start.

Not that it seemed to be counting for much.

'Resume massage,' Mr Dawson ordered, and Holly was about to climb back on the bed when Daniel halted her.

'Hold on a moment.' He had his fingers in Paul's groin to feel for a femoral pulse. 'He's got a pulse.'

And then, better than any music, better than any other sound in the world really, the monitor started to deliver bleeps.

Two at first, followed by a long pause, then a run of three and then sinus rhythm kicked in and there was the beep-beep-beep of a rapid heart rate and suddenly there was hope.

It was tainted, though.

Paul had been down for some considerable time. The cardiologists were going through his ECG tracings and deciding whether to take him straight up to ICU or directly to the catheter lab to see exactly what had occurred. The hope was that they could dissolve the blockage and open up the blocked vessels in Paul's heart and minimise damage to the heart muscle.

'I'll go up with him,' Kay said, as she gathered up the necessary equipment for the urgent transfer. 'Daniel, can you go and speak with Nora and explain that Mr Dawson is busy with Paul but he'll be in to get the consent…' Her voice trailed off. 'You know the drill.'

'I do.'

'I forget how experienced you are.'

'That's fine,' Daniel responded with ease, but then he asserted himself—not just with Kay but also with the cardiologist who would like Paul up in the lab, preferably ten minutes ago. 'First of all, though, we need to bring in his wife.'

'Time is of the essence,' Mr Dawson said.

'I'm sure she'll understand that.'

Nora must have been getting ready for the party and chatting to Paul as she did so, with no idea as to what was about to come. One of her eyes was made up with glittery eye shadow and the other was not.

Seeing someone so visibly shaken who was always so together and strong, but doing her best to hold it together, had Holly on the edge of tears.

'He's going to go up very soon,' Holly told Nora quietly, once Mr Dawson had obtained her consent and explained that they'd be moving him to the catheter lab. Holly watched as Nora took one of Paul's hands and held it in both of hers as if trying to warm it.

'He was telling me he'd just hidden my Christmas present.' Nora looked at Paul as she spoke. 'Please, don't leave me,' she asked him, and then, looking at Holly, said, 'I knew the day I met him that he was the one. He took a couple of weeks to get used to the idea…'

Holly didn't know what to say.

What was there to say to add to a love that had lasted for more than thirty years?

And so instead of saying the right thing, Holly found herself wearing her nervous smile.

Thankfully, Nora knew her well enough not to take offence.

'I just need a minute alone with him,' Nora said.

Holly nodded as Anna popped her head around the curtain. 'Nora, your daughter wants to come in.'

'No.' Nora was firm. 'She's too upset and she'd just distress him.'

Kay nodded her head and called for Holly to come the other side of the curtain, leaving Nora with Paul and the anaesthetist. Holly had turned up the volume on the monitors so that the staff could move in quickly if there was any change.

And they listened as Nora told her husband she loved him and to stay strong and that she'd be waiting for him once the procedure was done, and she did it all in a voice that did not waver, just in case Paul could hear.

Holly knew that voice only too well.

She could remember her mother going in for surgery and, because Holly was the only remotely medical person in the family, all questions had been aimed at her. All decisions had been run by Holly too and it had felt overwhelming. Her father had asked her to come with them up to Theatre. When he had started to break down it had been Holly who had stepped in. Holly had concentrated on keeping her smile in place while trying to ignore the fact that her mother was so very weak and frail from the chemotherapy and doing her best not to reveal that she wasn't terrified for her.

'What do you think?' Kay asked Daniel, and Holly looked at his grim face.

'They're giving him every chance.' His response was noncommittal but for Holly it said enough—he didn't think things looked good.

The quiet start had turned into a very busy shift and it didn't relent.

Holly felt all shaken but there was no time to sit down and reflect on what had happened. There was no pause button in Emergency, especially when you needed one.

Just as Paul left, another critically ill patient came in.

Kay handed Paul over to the care of the catheter lab staff but, given she was officially off duty, remained with Nora in the waiting room there. Holly was so busy that she had forgotten completely she was going out tonight and frowned when she saw that it was eight and that the night staff were starting to arrive.

'What are you doing here?' Holly asked.

'So you can leave early for the Christmas party.' Gloria grinned and then saw Holly's serious face. 'What is it?'

And there was no point in not telling the arriving staff—one look at the admissions board and they would see the truth for themselves.

'Nora's husband was brought in...'

As she brought the night staff up to speed Holly admitted that she had changed her mind about going to the party tonight, but Kay had other ideas. She had popped down to Emergency for that very reason, in fact, and called Holly round to her office.

'I need you to give the landlord the cash we've been collecting,' Kay said. They'd all been putting into the collection for a few weeks. 'Holly, I know the last thing you feel like is partying but word is already getting out about Paul. Nora's daughter has put it up on social media and honestly...' Kay let out a long sigh. 'Nora wants the party to go ahead. She thinks if it's called off now it means that we've given up on Paul.'

Holly nodded. 'How is he doing?'

'He's over on Intensive Care. He's in an induced coma and really we shan't know for a few days. Oh, I don't know, Holly, I don't have a very good feeling about it. He was down for a long time.'

'Less than an hour,' Holly pointed out.

'I know but...'

Kay looked as if she was about to cry and Holly had no idea what to say so she offered the only thing she knew might help. 'Do you want a cup of tea?'

Kay laughed the simplicity of Holly's solution and then she let out a little sob. 'I do,' she admitted. 'A quick one and then I'll head back up there. Have one with me?'

Holly brought in a tray as Kay got the envelope from the safe.

'I'd better not lose it,' Holly said, peering inside.

'You'd better not!' Kay barked, and then closed her eyes and leant back in her chair. 'It's nice to relax for five minutes.'

'Did you call Eamon and let him know?' Holly asked, referring to Kay's husband.

'I did. He's going to come and get me when I'm ready but I think I should stay awhile. Poor Nora. Honestly, that family of hers...' Kay rolled her eyes. 'Do you know? Her daughter asked what was going to happen for dinner! Does she not know how a bloody vending machine works? Fancy bothering her mother with that?'

'And fancy bothering you with this,' Daniel said, as he knocked on the half-open door.

'What do you want?' Kay asked. But as Daniel came in, though he gave Kay a smile, he then looked at Holly as he spoke.

'All the night staff are here but Laura is having no luck getting a taxi. The wait is an hour at best. I said that I could drop you all off at the end of my shift, which is right about now.'

'Then you'd better get ready,' Kay said, moving to stand. 'And I'd better get back up to Nora.'

'Finish your tea,' Holly suggested, and thought of the times she had sat with her own family, waiting for news, and how utterly exhausting it was. 'Have a few moments to yourself.'

'I might just do that,' Kay agreed. 'You're not on tomorrow, are you?'

'No, I'm off now till Monday, but I'll call in the morning and see how Paul's doing and—' Her voice halted abruptly as Holly stopped herself from saying what she had been about to—fancy bothering Kay with a stupid thing like the off duty while Paul was so sick, but Nora had been the one practically keeping the off duty running over the Christmas break.

It could wait, Holly knew that, and felt guilty for even considering raising it now.

So instead of worrying about tomorrow, or the next, or the next, she went into the changing room and had the quickest shower ever. There was just time for a dart under the jets and a quick soap and rinse then she dried herself and pulled on her little black dress.

'That's nice,' Anna said as Holly came out. Anna was hogging the one tiny mirror and applying eyeliner, while looking stunning in a very slinky, very red dress. 'You *always* look good in that.'

It was such a backhanded compliment that Holly actually stopped in her tracks for a second, before sitting down on the bench and pulling out her make-up bag.

'Thanks.' Holly smiled, pretending she had missed the rather bitchy comment. Oh, she was in no mood for make-up but it was certainly needed! As well as that the steam, even from a very brief shower, had made her curly hair even more so.

'Daniel's waiting,' Anna said rather pointedly as she turned from the mirror, all ready, just as Holly got her mascara out. 'We don't really have much time.'

'Daniel can wait for five minutes,' Holly answered. She hadn't asked him to play taxi driver and, more to the point, she wouldn't have minded the long wait for a taxi just to be able to get ready and allow for some time to jolt herself out of her morose mood. 'Or you guys can go on without me and I'll see you there.'

'No need for that. I'll go and wait with Daniel,' Anna said.

'Sure.'

'I'll see if I can persuade him to stay for a drink. After all, it is effectively his leaving do.'

'It's been Daniel's leaving do since October,' Holly said. There was a knot of disquiet in her stomach, though, at the thought she might not see him again but Anna merely shrugged.

'Then I might just have to kiss him goodbye!'

Holly, whether she liked Anna or not, was genuinely curious. 'Doesn't it bother you that he'll be gone soon?'

'Any one of us could be gone soon.' Anna shrugged. 'If working here doesn't prove that, then I don't know what will. I intend to enjoy every moment.'

And Anna was off. Teetering out on skinny legs and high heels and leaving that thought hanging in the air as heavily as her perfume.

Finally Holly had a moment alone.

She leant her head against the wall and closed her eyes and thought not just of Nora and Paul but of her own parents.

This time last year had been fraught, with Holly accompanying her mother to appointments and dashing to be there on her days off to offer support.

Tomorrow, after she'd done some shopping, Holly would be back on the motorway and again headed for home.

One year on it felt as if not much had changed. And in a year where there had been a rather marked absence of fun, in the latter months Daniel had somehow brightened her days.

She was, very possibly, never going to see him again, and that *wasn't* the reason for the sudden threat of tears, Holly told herself. No, it had been an emotional shift and it was coming to the end of a difficult year.

That was why she was suddenly teary.

It had nothing to do with lost opportunities.

Had there even been any? Holly pondered as she sat there and thought back over their time. Yes, there had certainly been a few occasions where a little flirt could have maybe spilled into more.

But to what end?

Maybe she needed a more generous dose of Anna's thinking instead of her usual caution where men were concerned.

Or maybe, Holly conceded as she put on her coat and walked out of the changing room, she was just looking for an excuse to misbehave.

She made her way through the department.

There was Daniel looking all sexy in black jeans and

a really thin jumper that almost looked silky and the fabric was so thin that she could see his nipples.

Talk about *Think Like a Man*.

'Are you coming after all?' Holly asked, seeing that he looked dressed for, well, anything.

'No. Why?'

'Because you've changed.'

'I've changed because I'm a locum,' Daniel pointed out. 'If I didn't throw my scrubs in the linen skip at the end of my shift I'd have quite a collection at my flat by now from the various hospitals I've worked at.'

As they walked past the nurses' station he retrieved his Advent calendar. 'Do you want yours?' he said.

'Yes.' Holly said, and smiled at Gloria. 'I don't trust the night staff a bit.'

She added it to her bag, which she would lock up with her coat at the pub.

Really, she would far prefer to be on her way home than heading off to a party, especially one that Daniel wasn't attending.

They walked out of the hospital and towards his car. It was one of those cold, damp nights and Holly was glad she hadn't made any attempt to tame her hair.

So was Daniel.

He was used to seeing it tied back and wrestling its way out of confinement, but now it fell in a dark cloud past her shoulders and some curls fell forward as she stopped for a moment and checked inside her bag.

He had seen her out of uniform before—arriving at work in jeans—but he had never seen Holly dressed up before and he found himself wanting to know what she wore under that coat.

They fell into step as they walked towards the car

and it was Anna who asked the question that was on Holly's mind.

'When do you fly?'

'I haven't booked it yet,' Daniel answered. 'Probably next week.'

'Where are you going first?'

'Switzerland.'

He aimed his keys at a black car, which lit up, and then everyone loaded their bags into the boot and then piled in, Laura and Holly in the back, Anna in the front, and suddenly Daniel knew that one of the reasons he wasn't indulging in a little *après ski* right about now was Holly.

Several hospitals had called, asking him to work, and the answer had been no. It was only when a shift had come up in the emergency department at The Primary that he had accepted a shift.

And now, as everyone climbed into his car and Anna got in the front, it felt wrong—as if Holly should be the one in his front passenger seat.

Holly felt the same.

It was odd and it was with absolutely no reason, yet Holly found that she resented the way Anna had jumped in the front. Holly sat behind Anna and when Daniel turned his head to reverse out, for a moment their eyes met. Holly was tempted to wind down the window because it had suddenly become very warm in the car and the heater had barely gone on.

Daniel moved the car out of the parking spot and then drove to the barrier and swiped his ID card. There he glanced in the rear-view mirror, not to check for traffic, more to see if her eyes were waiting.

They were.

All too often she averted her gaze, failing to complete what they started.

Not tonight.

Holly hoped it was dark enough that he couldn't see she was blushing and then a car tooted behind them.

'Daniel,' Anna prompted, because although the barrier was up the car hadn't moved.

'Sorry,' Daniel said. 'I was miles away.'

In bed with Holly!

'Everyone's asking about Paul,' Laura said, going through the messages on her phone. 'What do we say?'

'As little as possible,' Daniel suggested.

They were on the main road now and he glanced back into the mirror but Holly was now looking out of the window, watching the world go by and lost in thoughts of her own,

She liked Daniel far, far too much, Holly knew.

There was nothing wrong with liking someone except she wasn't wired like Anna. For Holly it would be foolish at best to get involved with a man who was days away from leaving the country.

Except she already was.

In her head Holly was already involved and yet she had not a single memory to draw from.

Was it time to change that?

'We're here.' Laura nudged her and Holly wiped the steamed-up window and looked out at the pub—a regular venue for Emergency dos. They often hired a room at the back and a lot of good times had been had there.

'Come in for one,' Anna said to Daniel, and Holly felt her skin prickle because Anna could flirt for England and she was seriously flirting now.

'I'm driving.'

Holly's eyes went to the mirror and again met his. Both of them knew that she would usually have looked away or been halfway out of the car by now.

'Come on,' Anna pushed, oblivious to the current coming from behind. 'You might enjoy yourself.'

'You know, I think I might,' Daniel said.

And so, instead of them climbing out, Daniel drove to the car park at the rear. It was packed but he found a space and soon they were all walking to the pub.

All except Holly, who was still by the car and going through her bag.

'What are you doing?' Daniel asked her because since they'd left Emergency he had seen her go through her bag many times.

'Compulsively checking that I've still got the envelope that Kay gave me.' Holly said. 'I have to pay the landlord…'

They went in the main entrance and there was the lovely pub scent but mixed with the woody smell of a fire in the entrance, and Holly felt her cheeks go pink for no other reason than it was lovely and warm.

The women all handed over their coats and their hands were all stamped so that they could get in and out of the function room. As Laura and Anna went through Holly asked where she should put the bar money.

'You'll need to see Desmond,' she was told, and was pointed in the right direction. 'He's in the lounge bar.'

'Thanks.'

'I'll come with you,' Daniel offered, and Holly nodded.

It had been well worth coming in, Daniel decided, for under Holly's coat she was wearing a black velvet dress, or rather it was raven. As he walked behind her Daniel noted the deep blue hue shimmering on the curves of her hips. Holly's legs were dressed in very sheer stockings and her heels were high, and as he moved forward to hold open the door, Daniel resisted placing his hand on the small of her back to guide her in.

Holly already felt as if he had, for her spine felt warm and her bottom too big, just from the burn of his gaze.

Desmond wasn't there, but they waited at the bar while one of the staff tracked him down.

It was a lovely old pub and there was a pine Christmas tree that was beautifully decorated and its scent filled the room.

'Christmassy enough for you?' Daniel asked.

'It's lovely.' Holly smiled but it was a bit of a forced one.

'Are you not in the mood for a party?' Daniel said, toying with the idea of suggesting they skip it when Holly nodded.

'I feel awful.'

'He might be okay.'

'No, I feel awful because...' She shook her head.

And then, for Daniel, something rather untoward happened—instead of wondering how quickly they could dispense with the small talk and get in the car and back to his, he actually wanted to hear what Holly had to say and *then* get back to the essentials.

'Tell me.'

'No,' Holly said, but then her guilty conscience demanded full disclosure. 'You know Kay was saying how, when they were waiting outside the catheter lab, Nora's daughter asked her what was for dinner...'

Daniel laughed a black laugh, it was nothing he hadn't seen with relatives.

'I'm as bad,' Holly said.

'Why, did you demand that Nora feed you?'

'No.' Holly smiled but then it changed. 'I almost asked Kay what would happen to the off duty for Christmas.' It had worried at her all evening. 'I mean, Paul's lying there half-dead, and I'm stressing over the off duty.'

'I'm quite sure Kay is.'

'I doubt it,' Holly sighed. 'Nora and she are best friends.'

'Off the record?' Daniel said, and Holly nodded.

'Kay's words to me just before she headed off to the catheter lab, and I quote, "How the feck am I going to sort out the roster now?"'

'Really?' Holly laughed.

'Really.' Daniel nodded. 'And I bet Nora, if Paul is now stable, is worrying about the million and one things that you women seem to worry about at this time of year.'

'That's very sexist.'

'Just an observation.'

'A wrong one.'

'I can only go by what I've seen. My father never did a thing for Christmas, I aim to be far away from it...' He thought for a moment. 'My uncle leaves it all to my aunt...'

Desmond came along then and he took the money and wrote out a receipt, which Holly put in her purse for Kay. 'What can I get you?' he offered. 'On the house, before you go in to that mad lot.'

Oh.

'I'll just have a soda water, thanks.' Daniel said.

'Well, he's a cheap date.' Desmond smiled at Holly. 'What can I get you?'

'I'd love a Scotch, please.'

She really, really would.

Holly wasn't a big drinker at the best of times but a lovely Scotch felt about right and Daniel motioned to a table near an open fire and the tree and they took a seat there.

'Maybe I am in the mood for Christmas after all.' Holly smiled, sitting back in the chair and relaxing to the lovely crackle of the fire and inhaling the scent of her drink.

'I want one,' Daniel admitted.

'Tough.' Holly smiled and then took a sip, enjoying the burn of the liquor. 'I don't really like spirits but my dad loves Scotch so I always keep a bottle at home and every now and then I have one.'

'Well, that's good to know.'

'What?'

He smiled and she realised he was perhaps inviting himself to her home for a drink.

Or had she been inviting him?

Hmm.

Holly still didn't know where this might lead, but it was just so nice to be out in the real world with him and without buzzers and patients and others around. And it was definitely nice to squeeze in five minutes' pause after work before they headed into the party.

'Do you get on with your parents?' he asked.

'Very much so.'

'They live…?' Daniel frowned. He wasn't sure, though he knew that it was some distance that she often travelled to get home.

'Up north,' Holly said, and then told him the village where her family lived.

'So how come you're in London?'

'Because I get on so well with my family.' Holly smiled. 'I trained up there and it was all too easy to just live at home… I knew I needed a change.'

'Yet you're still home a lot?'

'My mum hasn't been very well.' Holly said, and decided the night had already been grim enough without going further into it. 'What about you? Are your family in London?'

She didn't know him at all, Daniel realised.

Holly could have no idea just how refreshing that was. Even before he had started medicine there had been a constant stream of 'Marcus Chandler's son'. His father had been head boy at the boarding school Daniel had attended and his record was just as impressive at med school and beyond. Even Kay had made a few comments and had asked if he was any relation to the esteemed Professor Chandler.

Holly had no idea as to that side of his life.

'Yes.' Daniel answered the question as to whether his family was in London very simply.

'Do you get on?'

'Nope,' Daniel said.

'Why?'

'Because my father is an arrogant git,' he said, and then looked at her Scotch. 'Given that I'm on soda water tonight, I shan't be sharing.'

Holly laughed. 'What about your mother?'

'She's dead.'

Well, that wiped the smile from her face.

'He married again. I've got a sister...'

Daniel refused to call Maddie a half-sister.

'Do you get on with her?'

'I do when I see her. And that reminds me, I must get her a Christmas present before I head off.'

Holly's phone buzzed, indicating an incoming text, and she glanced down and saw that it was Anna, asking where they had disappeared to.

'Has our absence been noted?' Daniel asked.

'It has.'

The pleasant interlude was over but it had been nice,

Holly thought as she drained her drink and then stood. It had been a tiny but very welcome pause before she pushed out a smile and faced the masses.

He knew it was pointless suggesting that they didn't go through.

Holly took her Christmas party as seriously as her decorations.

'Time to be positive...' Holly said, though she didn't really feel it. 'It *is* Christmas and if ever there was a time for miracles...'

'Please,' Daniel scorned, pouring a bucket of iced water on that. 'There's no such thing as Christmas miracles.'

'Are you always so negative?' Holly asked as they headed towards the function room.

'Always.'

The doors swung open and there were a few shouts of 'Holly!' but there were a lot more shouts of Daniel's name! Clearly a lot of women were very glad to see him.

Anna, of course, leapt to his side and handed him an elaborate-looking cocktail.

'I'm driving,' he pointed out again.

'It a virgin.' Anna smiled. 'I had it prepared just for you.'

Oh, please. Holly thought she might spit at the suggestive tone, but she refused to be rattled by Anna. Instead, she put on her smile and chatted with friends.

It was a difficult night. Everyone wanted first-hand information and Holly knew that wasn't her place to give it. It was up to Nora what she wanted to share and for now Nora wanted upbeat and so that's what Holly did her best to be, but by ten she was done.

She looked over and Anna and Daniel were locked in conversation.

Or rather Anna was conversing and Daniel was locked, given the slight eye roll that he gave her.

Holly smiled but it was a regretful one because she simply didn't know how to run wild. How to go over there and be all sparkling and witty and flirt…

Except, as it turned out, she didn't have to go over there to flirt. Holly quickly realised that standing in the middle of the room and blatantly staring at the object of your desire seemed to work rather well too!

Yikes.

She hadn't meant that!

Holly watched as he said something to Anna and Holly realised he was excusing himself and about to make his way over.

It was time for a quick getaway.

'You're not going already?' Trevor, one of the male nurses, asked.

'I am.' Holly kept up that smile. 'I'm hitting the shops tomorrow and then…' She didn't finish. An absolute novice in the field of sexual adventure, she found her coat and headed outside.

'Leaving?'

She turned and there was Daniel.

'Yes.'

'Do you want a lift?'

'I've just called for a taxi,' Holly lied.

'It's no problem.'

'I live miles away.'

'I'll save you the fare, then.'

'No, thanks.'

Why? Holly asked herself. Why was she saying no? Because she *couldn't* say no to him.

'Come on.'

He jangled his keys and Holly nodded. Really, it was

just a colleague giving her a lift home and it would be bliss not to have to make small talk with a taxi driver or sit in the back as he chatted on his phone.

Liar, liar.

They got in his car, and this time she was in the front.

That's better, both thought but didn't say.

'Address?' he asked, and she gave it to him.

Daniel typed it into his phone and that took care of that, and then he started the engine.

'Head north,' his phone said.

'I hate that,' Daniel admitted. 'I have no idea which way north is. I need a compass in the middle of my steering wheel.'

'She means turn left,' Holly said.

'Thank you.'

'Are you all packed?' Holly made a feeble attempt at small talk and he nodded.

'Sort of. I'm trying to rent out my flat. Apparently December isn't an ideal time to find tenants.'

'So it that why your plans keep changing?'

'In part.'

'Well, you might just as well stick around for Christmas…'

'I doubt it. I might even fly out then, it's just another day.'

'You don't mean that.'

'I do,' Daniel said, and he gave her a smile. 'We're polar opposites.' And then he stared ahead at the road and it did not need stating—that opposites attracted.

Both already knew.

CHAPTER THREE

SHE SHOULD HAVE said goodbye to him back at the pub.

Then there might have been a hope that, should they meet up in the future, all they would be were ex-colleagues who had flirted a little on occasion.

Back at the pub she could have wished him well for his trip and, yes, of course she could do the same when he pulled up at her flat.

Holly didn't want to, though.

How did it even work? Holly thought. She was way too far out of her comfort zone. Did she offer him a drink, or did she leave it to him to suggest coming in?

And what about the morning?

Holly wished that she didn't overthink things, she wished she could be more like Anna and just worry about the day, or rather the night, at hand.

She wanted the traffic lights to turn red, for a pause, to turn and tell him that the flirty version of Holly he had met at times wasn't the real one. That the woman who had laughed at the suggestive tone in his voice when he'd told her she'd be in discreet hands, did not, prior to his arrival on her part of the planet, exist.

Yet the lights all stayed green and afforded swift passage.

And anyway, Daniel knew all that.

While he was driving he was trying to convince himself that this wasn't any different from what he was used to and that Holly could more than handle a hook-up. And he was also trying to convince himself that he didn't care in the way he actually did.

He couldn't afford to care. It wasn't an emotion he sought, and he was leaving after all.

His phone told him that the destination was on his left and he slid the car into a parking space outside her flat and his conscience won—Daniel didn't want to risk hurting her.

'You'd better go in,' Daniel said.

And so this was it.

'Thanks for the lift.'

'No problem.'

'It's been nice working with you,' Holly said. 'I'm going to miss your sulking face.'

'I'll miss your smiling one.'

And this really was it.

There was a charge in the air that should signal thunder but instead Daniel turned and looked ahead.

Holly reached to open the door and he did nothing to halt her so she got out.

They were both congratulating themselves on how adult and sensible they had been.

Now she could breathe, except, despite the cool and the drizzle, the night felt as humid as if it was summer.

Holly looked at the path to her door and she was six, maybe seven steps away from saving herself from a rather big mistake, except she wanted so badly to turn around and to follow desire rather than walk away.

Just once.

It was her choice as to what happened next, Holly knew.

Could she keep it light, without revealing how deeply she felt?

Daniel was just about to hit 'Home' as his destination when she tapped on the window.

'What?' he asked as it slid down. His voice was surly. He didn't want to do this a second time, especially as now that she was bending down there was the pearly white of her breasts at eye level.

And she looked at him and, no, she would not be so cheesy as to ask him in for a drink and then somehow, whoops, they'd up in bed.

She wanted a kiss, Daniel knew, but he was also rather certain she wanted a whole lot more than that. Not just sex, but the part of himself he refused to give.

'What?' he said again, and then his face broke into a smile, as, very unexpectedly, Holly, sweet Holly, showed another side of her.

'Are you going to *make* me invite you in?'

'Yes.'

'You're not even going to try and persuade me with a kiss?' Holly checked.

'You want me or you don't.' Daniel shrugged. 'There's no question that I want you. But, Holly, do you get that—?'

She knew what was coming and she didn't need the warning—he had made his position perfectly clear—so she interrupted him. 'I don't need the speech.'

She just needed this.

Holly had thought his hand was moving to open the door but instead it came out of the window and to her head and pulled her face down to his.

He kissed her hard, even though she was the one standing. The stubble of his unshaven jaw was rough on her face and his tongue was straight in.

He pulled her in tight so that her upper abdomen hurt from the pressure of the open window and it was a warning, she knew, of the passion to come.

Even now she could pull back and straighten, say goodnight and walk off, but Holly was through with being cautious.

In a second she would be falling through the open window for all the neighbours to see and sucked into the dark vacuum of his car.

Holly simply didn't care.

Her bag dropped to the pavement and he then released her.

Holly stared back at him, breathless, her lipstick smeared across her face, and all it made him want to do was to kiss her again.

But this was a street.

Holly bent and retrieved her bag and then walked off towards her flat. There was a roaring sound in her ears and her heart seemed to be leaping up near her throat.

Daniel closed up the car and was soon following her to the flats.

She turned the key in the main door to the flats and clipped up the concrete steps.

She could hear his heavy footsteps coming up the steps behind her as she turned and Holly almost broke into a run.

Daniel actually did!

He had thought her cute, sweet and gorgeous these past months and had done all he could not to think of her outright as sexy.

Except she was, and seriously so.

Those heavy footsteps chasing her were thrilling and caught up with her just as she was getting her key into the door of her own flat. Holly was breathless with excitement and the rush and power of him grabbing for her almost toppled Holly as they burst in through the door.

The hall was in darkness; he could just make out some Christmas-tree lights in a room down the hall but there was no time to get to the lounge.

Daniel had no patience now.

Holly had never known anything like it. Never, in her almost twenty-nine years, had she had that simply-have-to-have-you feeling.

And Daniel *had* to have her.

Every obstacle he dealt with.

He hitched her lovely raven dress up.

Stockings?

No problem, he expertly removed them and then her knickers too.

And when he wanted a better view of her breasts he lowered her zipper at the back, just enough to free them.

Holly looked down at her exposed breasts, and then at her stockings and knickers lying on the hallway floor— she felt slutty and sexy. She liked it. So much so that she was pulling at his thin jumper just to reveal his stomach, and then running a hand up the heavy jeans-clad thighs, getting closer to the lovely bit in the middle. She dealt with the brass button deftly, though she broke a nail on the zipper, and then freed him. He was clearly as keen and eager as she, and Holly was so utterly ready for him she nearly forgot about condoms.

To Holly's mind there was nothing sexy about condoms, but he changed that in an instant, for he pulled out his wallet, found one, tossed the wallet to the floor and tore the foil with his teeth.

'Put it on,' Daniel told her, and he started to squeeze and play with her breasts as she did just that.

She rolled it down slowly, which was quite a feat,

given the way his fingers were exploring her, and she felt the jerk of impatience in her hand.

Then he said the two little words that tonight she was desperate to hear.

'Get on.'

Gladly she did.

He bent his knees just enough that he could thrust into her and Holly's shoulders hit the wall. She arched back at the consuming pleasure as he stabbed inside her.

Totally consumed and controlled by him, Holly was close to coming as Daniel lifted her legs even further; she wrapped them around his hips.

'I've been wanting you all night.' He told her as she wrapped her legs tighter, wiggling herself down further so he could push deeper. 'I wanted you on sight.'

They stared at each other as he banged her into wall, kissing her with raw passion and digging his fingers into her bottom, holding her firm. Heat flooded her centre and she moved her mouth away. 'I'm going to come...'

Her voice divulged her own surprise. Not just because she usually took for ever, more because of the intensity that hit.

Daniel felt her gather and pull tight around him as he plunged one last time before letting go deep inside her.

He lowered her down and she stood a moment on legs that felt she was getting over a bout of the flu they were so weak.

They followed the Christmas-tree lights to what he assumed was the lounge.

Maybe he'd get that Scotch after all, Daniel thought.

Instead, they collapsed onto her bed.

'Holly?'

The room had stopped spinning and they lay on their

backs on the bed when Daniel started to take in his sur-
roundings. 'Why is there a Christmas tree in your bedroom?'

'My neighbours are a bit noisy,' Holly explained. 'And
so I tend to spend more time in here.'

'Oh.'

'And it seemed a shame to have a Christmas tree in a
room that I don't spend much time in.'

They were half-undressed already so it took only a
moment to throw off the rest of their clothes and to get
into bed.

They lay talking, about nothing much as well as a lot.

And it turned out their paths had almost crossed.

'I went for an interview at the Royal when I was looking at moving to London.' She thought back to that time
and her nervousness as she'd entered the huge Victorian
building.

It was funny to think now that he might have been
inside.

'How long ago?'

'I was twenty-one,' Holly said. 'So eight, nearly nine
years ago. Were you there then?'

He nodded. 'Did you get the job?'

'Yes,' Holly said. 'But I got offered the job at The Primary in the same week and I chose to go there. I didn't
like how they rotated the staff at the Royal. Too many
night shifts.'

'Don't you like nights?'

'Not really,' Holly said. 'I don't sleep very well during the day.'

'I could have had you when you were twenty-one.'
Daniel mused, liking that idea.

'No, you couldn't have.' Holly smiled at his arrogant assumption. 'I was seeing someone then. I nearly got engaged.'

And he lay there, not liking that idea.

'We might have ended up having an affair,' Daniel said, determined to have had her at twenty-one in his head.

'No,' she said. 'We wouldn't have.'

And he lay there wondering why the hell he was sulking over an event that had never even taken place some eight or nine years ago!

'Why did you break up?'

'He got offered a job in America,' Holly said. 'I didn't want to go and he did. We were too young, I guess.'

They were heading into territory that Daniel generally avoided so they started chatting about work.

'I don't do well with grieving relatives,' Holly announced.

'Yes, you do.' He frowned because the few times he'd been with Holly while breaking bad news she'd always been fine.

If a little quiet.

'Oh, I'm better than I was,' Holly agreed. 'I have this nervous smile...'

And Daniel found that he was smiling as she spoke.

'I didn't know that I had it, well, I sort of did but then Kay had to take me to one side...'

'You smile at bad news?' Daniel checked.

'No, but I smile when I'm nervous. You should see me in my school photos and when I go for an interview and things...'

And there it was again.

This wanting to look at old photos.

To hear more.

To know more.

It was everything he was trying to resist.

* * *

Freezing.

Daniel woke to the cold air and warm bed and rolled into Holly.

God, she felt good.

Her soft bottom was against him and as his hand went over hers he kissed her bare shoulder and then his mouth moved up her neck.

Last night had been amazing.

Now he wanted more.

And so did Holly.

His hand lifted her hair and his kiss was heavy on her neck as light fingers circled her stomach.

But then he stopped.

Daniel actually stopped in mid-kiss because fast sexy sex was one thing, but the way he wanted her now could only serve to confuse Holly.

Arrogant assumption perhaps but he knew she liked him, seriously liked him, and he liked her enough not to want to give mixed messages.

And so how did you end things nicely?

Usually he didn't give it too much thought, for he generally played to a far tougher crowd.

Holly closed her eyes at the abrupt end to his kiss on her shoulder. They were both in that lovely turned-on morning feeling and she wanted to turn her face to his mouth, to kiss him slowly and make love.

Yes, that.

She wanted the hand that had been slowly stroking her stomach to resume its perusal and move lower yet it didn't.

Too intimate for you, Daniel? she wanted to say, though didn't, but she did get her own back a little because she slowly stretched and yawned, just so he could *feel* what he was missing, and then rolled over to face him and smiled.

Yes, she was nice but, oh, she could be wicked.

'It's so nice to have a weekend off.' Holly smiled and chatted as if she hadn't even noticed his erection.

'I've got every weekend off now.' Daniel smiled back as she gave him a small kick to let him know how unfair that was.

She was back to looking into those amazing eyes but from her pillow this time. 'Are you registering to practise overseas?' Holly asked.

'It's an option, I guess.' He couldn't tell her his plans because the truth was he didn't really have any. 'I just want to take a year and work things out.'

'Fair enough,' Holly said, but her slight frown told him that she didn't really get it. They truly were opposites, not just that he had made so few plans but also that he could afford to take a year off. Shouldn't he have worked this all out some time ago?

'I'll make coffee…' Daniel offered.

'I'll go,' Holly said. 'The machine's tricky.'

'I'm sure I can work it out.'

She lay there and wondered how this would end. Awkwardness was creeping in and she didn't know how to put on a brave smile when he left.

And then she heard her front door open and then quietly close.

'Bastard,' Holly breathed.

But then a moment or so later she heard the door open again and lay back on the pillows, recanting her curse as she realised he must have left the door on the latch so he could get back in.

Holly knew she was way out of her comfort zone here, so much so that she had actually thought he might just walk off without so much as a goodbye. Instead, though, he walked in with two mugs of coffee *and* two Advent calendars that he must have retrieved from the car. He put the drinks on the bedside tables and dropped the calendars on the bed.

'Holly, why don't you have any food in your fridge?'

'There are eggs.'

'But no bread,' he pointed out. 'I heard the neighbours, or rather I could hear breakfast television and her shouting for him to get up…'

'I told you,' Holly said. 'It's worse during the week. She must call to him about fifteen times before he surfaces. Sometimes I want to go round there and pull the duvet off him myself!'

And he would rather like to pull the duvet from her but instead he just climbed in.

She reached for the floor and handed out cushions so that they could sit up in comfort.

Her bedroom really was rather lovely. Even aside from the Christmas tree! There were books and a pile of DVDs lining shelves and a television on a chest of drawers. There was her computer and phone and, really, apart from the occasional trip to the bathroom or kitchen he could absolutely see why she might not want to leave. 'You could bring the coffee maker in here,' Daniel suggested.

'I did think of that…' Holly nodded '…but then I'd need a little fridge too…'

'And then you'd get bedsores,' Daniel said, and was about to make a little joke about having to roll her every couple of hours, but he knew where that would lead.

'I'd better go soon.'

'Good,' Holly said, 'because I've got a lot to do.'

She picked up her Advent calendar and started to peel off the Cellophane as Daniel tackled his.

'I can't believe you've never had one of these.'

'I might have when I was really little,' Daniel said. 'I honestly can't remember.'

For all his inexperience he found the number one before Holly did and was soon pulling out a small circle of dark chocolate from behind the little cardboard window.

'I doubt it's very good,' Holly warned as she too found hers. 'Given that Kay bought a job lot. Still, it's the thought...' Her voice trailed off as she popped it in her mouth. It was the darkest, sweetest and most melt-in-the-mouth chocolate she had ever tasted, and Daniel clearly felt the same since he was already opening door number two.

'Oh, my!' Holly said.

'Wait till you taste December the second,' Daniel warned. 'It's some orange liqueur...'

'I think I'm going to come!' Holly said as she rolled it around her tongue.

'Well, lucky for you, it's December the third now, so you can have another.'

The third was behind a little door with a gingerbread man on it and the chocolate was a coffee and cream.

'They get better and better,' Daniel said.

The chocolate was so seriously superb that Holly was very much considering breaking her own rule and just eating all twenty-five in one go.

'If that's the beginning of the month,' Daniel said, 'then what's behind those double doors...?' He turned the calendar over and read the fine print. 'It's from Belgium.'

'So what's it doing in the discount store?'

'We should go and buy up all that's left.' Daniel suggested.

'I'll have to find out which one she went to.'

Hot coffee soon washed down the chocolate but instead of Daniel heading for home and Holly to the shops they were back on their sides and facing each other.

'I'm starving,' Daniel said.

'There's a baker's across the street, they do really nice pastries.'

'Go on, then,' he said, but she shook her head.

'You go.'

And for someone who had been about to leave, Daniel was considering not just heading to the bakers on his way home but returning to her bed with a box of pastries.

'We could just go and get breakfast.' Daniel suggested the name of a very nice department store and as she licked her lips at the suggestion he waited for that ping of regret for prolonging things to descend in his chest, but it wasn't there. His only regret was that he might be leading her on, and yet, he reasoned, it was just breakfast.

'Sounds good,' Holly said. 'It has to be a quick breakfast, though…' She glanced at the time. 'I want to do some Christmas shopping.'

'And me.'

Daniel did, as he hadn't got anything for Maddie. She was already terribly disappointed that he wouldn't be there for Christmas and he hoped that it might be tempered by a lovely gift.

But what to get a five-year-old who has everything?

And whatever it was he would have to have it delivered. There was no way he was rocking up for Christmas dinner after the disaster of last year.

As he borrowed Holly's shower, Daniel told himself that the expedition he'd suggested was a terrible idea.

From sex to shopping?

And Holly was thinking the same, though along different lines, because as Daniel showered his phone rang and she looked at the screen and saw the name 'Maddie'.

Whoever Maddie was she was impatient, because she rang three times in the space of five minutes.

Holly tried not to mind.

Yet she did.

When he came out of the shower it was to the sight of Holly sitting on the bed and pulling on boots.

'I wish I'd done this before I put on my jeans,' Holly said and to Daniel it seemed there was nothing more on her mind than breakfast.

He picked up the phone and gave a small eye roll when he saw that there were a few missed calls from Maddie.

There often were!

He had a listen to check there wasn't a problem.

There wasn't.

'Hello, I've got your ticket for the nativity play.'

Next message. 'I'm an angel.'

And so on.

What on earth should he get her for Christmas?

'Let's go,' Holly said, trying to keep the edge from her voice as he blatantly listened to his messages. 'I think the café opens at ten.'

They arrived at a quarter past, which, as it turned out, was perfect timing because everyone who had been queuing for the café to open were pretty much served.

'I'll have the full English breakfast...' Daniel didn't even need to look at the menu.

'Well, I'm going to have mince pies and cream and a strong coffee.'

The fruit mix in the pie was warm and spicy and the cream sweet and it was the perfect breakfast really, although it had little to do with the food.

Despite their brief misgivings about their breakfast date, conversation was surprisingly easy.

Usually for Daniel the conversation ran out at first

kiss, or certainly by the time his head had hit the pillow, but Holly's company was just as pleasant this morning as it had been last night.

'Who do you have to buy for?' Holly asked as Daniel slathered brown sauce on his mushrooms.

'My sister.'

'Who else?'

'No one else. You?'

'Everyone!' Holly sighed and then took out her phone. 'But first I'm going to call work.'

'About Paul or the Christmas roster?'

'Stop!' Holly blushed. 'Don't you dare repeat that to anyone.'

'I never repeat pillow talk.'

'It was said in your car.'

'Yes, but by then you'd already made up your mind that you'd be hauling me into your lair.'

'No,' Holly said as she made the call, and having asked the switchboard operator to put her through to Kay she smiled at him. 'That was a last-minute decision.'

'I'm glad you made it.'

So too was she, Holly thought as she returned to her phone call.

'Kay, it's Holly.'

'He's stable, no real change, but that's good.' Kay got straight to it. 'No arrhythmias overnight but they'll keep him intubated for a couple of days.'

'How's Nora?'

'Exhausted. She's just gone home for a sleep. How was the party?'

'It was good,' Holly said. 'Everyone was concerned about Paul, of course, but I think it went well.'

'I heard that you left early.'

'Well, I wasn't exactly in the mood...you know that.'

'I also heard Daniel didn't just drop you girls off but came in for a drink.'

'He did.'

'Hold on a moment.' Holly sat there and she heard Kay closing her office door and Holly sat holding her breath, wondering if their leaving together had been noted.

She didn't have to worry, Holly soon realised as Kay spoke on. 'Anna was all over him, apparently?'

'I didn't notice.'

'Get out of here,' Kay scoffed. She knew Holly was always up to date with goings-on, although Kay prided herself on being The One Who Knew. 'So, who did he leave with?'

Holly sat there, watching as Daniel mopped up the egg with a thick bit of buttery toast, and she should be relieved, really, that Kay didn't for a second think it might be with her.

'I don't think he was with anyone,' Holly said, and her voice came out a little too high.

Daniel looked up when he heard her strained voice and saw her very red cheeks and he could guess what was being asked so he mouthed a suggestion.

'Do you want me to speak to her?'

Holly laughed at the thought of Kay's shocked expression if she handed Daniel the phone but shook her head and looked away, hunching her shoulders so she could talk without seeing the object of her sins.

'Oh.' Kay sounded deflated at the lack of gossip but when Kay spoke on so too did Holly. 'I'm going to have to take a long hard look at the roster, Holly.'

'I know.'

'And you know that I'll try to accommodate everyone but I do have to be fair. There are mums with little ones who need their mum to be there at Christmas, but you know that I'll try to do my best for all my staff.'

'I do appreciate it.'

Holly hung up and as she did so Daniel gave her a thin smile. 'Off duty?'

She nodded.

'See, I told you it wouldn't take long. The real world always surfaces.'

And it was surfacing now because as she glanced at the time Holly knew if she had wanted to do her shopping and get to her parents' by dinnertime, then she needed to get going.

They finished up their food and wandered out, but instead of parting ways they looked at the floor plan.

'What does your sister like?' Holly asked.

'Elephants.'

'Oh.'

He didn't explain that Maddie was five.

In truth, Daniel was very touchy about the fact his sister could very well be his daughter. In fact, when they were out together they were always mistaken as such.

They joined the swarms of people all looking for the perfect gift that would make another happy.

There was no such thing, Daniel knew.

Holly swallowed when he held up a necklace with an ugly-looking elephant hanging on the chain, Of course she assumed Daniel's sister was close to his age, and she found that she was wearing her nervous smile, which she quickly righted and then made a suggestion.

'Why don't you adopt an elephant for her?'

Daniel rolled his eyes.

'If I loved elephants,' Holly said, 'it would be the perfect gift.'

And then she found *her* perfect gift!

It was beach glass, all wired and knotted together into the most fantastic necklace and earrings.

'I should get this for Adam,' Holly said, 'though it's a bit pricey.'

'Adam?'

'My brother.'

'Right,' Daniel said, to show he had no problem with all of that. 'Right! It's very nice.'

'The necklace would be for me, Daniel.' Holly smiled at his attempt to be PC. 'After too many disasters we now buy what we really want for ourselves and wrap it, though it's from the other.'

'I see.'

He didn't.

Daniel knew very little of family traditions and the little things that others seemed to do so seamlessly to make Christmas Day special.

But then, in the middle of a department store and completely out of the blue, he remembered something. He had woken up and there was this lumpy sock at the end of his bed and there was some fruit in it but also a tiny miniature of a castle. A castle he knew because they had been on holiday there that summer.

The holiday wasn't really a memory, more that the castle he had held in his palm that morning was, for he had looked at it in the gift shop.

His mum must have done that, Daniel realised. She must have bought it then and saved it for Christmas. Certainly it wouldn't have been his father.

He just stood in the busy department store, remembering something from a long time ago.

Something precious.

'Why are they queuing?' Holly nudged him and pulled him from introspection.

She had put down the necklace and looked up to see a long line forming towards the back of the store.

'Because they've got nothing better to do.' Daniel shrugged. 'Maybe it's to see Santa.'

'But they're mainly adults,' Holly pointed out.

'Maybe it's an adult-rated Santa,' he suggested, but Holly didn't smile at his joke. 'You don't approve?'

'I refuse to buy into your constant downgrading of the magic of Christmas. I want to know what they're queuing for,' Holly said, and they made their way over to see what was going on.

No, it wasn't Santa and neither was it an adult Santa. It was really rather amazing. They clearly weren't the only ones who thought so because and if the queue was big, so too was the crowd gathered at the end of the line, watching what was being made.

A little elf, okay, a person dressed up as a little elf, was typing on a miniature keyboard. Further down the line a tiny stamp-sized letter was printed. There another elf was placing the tiny letters in equally small envelopes.

It took a moment to work out that the letters were being placed within hand-blown Christmas-tree decorations.

They both stood and watched the glassblower and time really did run away that morning because it was simply fascinating to watch.

Once made and cooled another group of elves then decorated the glass bauble and added a silver chain to hang it from the tree and then it was placed in a gorgeous box that was tied with a heavy silver bow.

'What a beautiful gift,' Holly said, although Daniel, though interested, was too practical to be convinced.

'I don't get it,' Daniel admitted. 'You'd have to break the glass to read the letter.'

'That's the whole point,' Holly said. 'You don't break the glass. Or maybe you do...'

They were debating this when someone called his name.

'Daniel!'

They both turned and walking towards them was a rather beautiful woman around Holly's age but light years ahead in style. She had long straight honey-brown hair that fell immaculately and she looked as if she had just stepped out of a make-up salon, though it was subtly done, of course. She wore neat grey trousers and boots and had on a thin coat and she was one of those people who couldn't spill something on themselves if they tried.

Her cheeks were pink, though, and starting to fire up like a sunset as Daniel said her name.

'Hi, Amelia.' He responded to her greeting with a rather terse nod. 'How are you?'

'Busy,' she admitted, and held up a couple of shopping bags. 'I'm just trying to get a few things...'

'I see.'

It was all rather tense and uncomfortable and when Amelia looked over at Holly, clearly expecting to be introduced, Daniel said nothing.

How did you? Daniel wondered. Did he turn to Holly and say, *Oh, Holly this is my stepmother.*

He hadn't seen her in almost a year.

Not since last Christmas Day, when Amelia had had rather too much drink and had told Daniel that, though the money was nice, the marriage wasn't great. He had woken from a doze on the sofa to be told by Amelia that she was tired of sleeping with an older man and wanted the younger version—his son, namely Daniel.

And no one would ever have to know.

Daniel had got up, got his jacket and gone home, and hadn't seen Mommy Dearest since.

'So what are you up to?' Amelia asked.

'Not much.'

Those two words crushed Holly.

He could have said Christmas shopping, Holly thought, or that they had just been and had breakfast. No, she didn't want him to go into detail but to stand beside her and tell this woman 'Not much' had Holly's confidence shrink as if salt had been poured over it.

She stood there, wearing that stupid, nervous smile as they carried on talking while she was, at best, ignored.

'So what are you doing over Christmas?' Amelia asked him.

Avoiding you and my father, Daniel was tempted to answer, but his voice was its usual mixture of boredom and disinterest.

'I'm not sure,' Daniel said. 'Working or skiing.'

'I could have guessed it would be one of the two.' She gave a tight smile. 'I'd better get on.'

'Sure,' Daniel said.

Amelia walked off and now it was Holly and Daniel who stood in strained silence but the fun of watching the glassblower do his work had now left them.

Daniel glanced over his shoulder to make sure Amelia had gone.

Holly saw that he did and misinterpreted it as Daniel craning his neck for one lingering look and suddenly she didn't want to be here any more. She just did not want to stand beside a man whose mind was elsewhere. A man who couldn't even be bothered to introduce her and described their morning as 'Not much'. A man who listened to his voice messages from another woman straight after getting out of her bed.

He had come with a warning and, a little late perhaps, Holly chose to heed it.

It was time to put her big girl's blouse on and remember just what it was that she had agreed to—a one-night stand and then they parted ways.

This wasn't a date, no matter how much Holly wanted to convince herself of that. Neither was it the start of something. She'd agreed to abide by Daniel Chandler's standards last night, which meant they should have been over with several hours ago.

She made it now.

'I'm going to head off,' Holly said. 'I've got a lot to get and then I'm heading off to my parents'.'

'Sure.'

'Thanks for breakfast.' Holly smiled.

'You're welcome.'

There was a very good chance that she'd never see him again, Holly knew that. *And so how did you end it?* she wondered. *Did you say, Have a nice life? Did you kiss the other on the cheek when you went your separate ways? Or did you just give a sort of half-wave and then walk off?*

Holly chose the latter.

CHAPTER FOUR

HOME.

Holly had rung ahead to say she'd be late and just before seven she exited the motorway and saw the lights of her village in the distance.

There was no sense of relief at being at her parents', though. In truth, it had been ages since she'd had a full weekend off and it would have been nice to catch up with some friends. Or rather, given the turn of events, it would have been nice to spend a night in alone and watch a movie and dwell on what had happened with Daniel. Still, her mum wanted some help getting things ready for Christmas and so instead of being morose Holly waved to her mum as she got out of the car and smiled brightly as she headed up the path.

Inside, the tree was up and the decorations were all out, so her father had clearly been busy. Her mother went back into the kitchen to finish off making dinner and Holly went in to give her a hand.

'We waited for you,' Esther said.

'I told you not to,' Holly replied, because she'd told them to go ahead and eat.

The sound of the electric knife filled the room for a moment but when it went silent Holly knew that she ought to give her mother fair warning so she spoke. 'Mum, there might be a change to the off duty over Christmas.'

'I thought it had all been done.' Esther turned and then looked at the calendar on the fridge. 'You're off from the twenty-third till the twenty-eighth.'

'I was supposed to be but a couple of people have gone off sick and…' Holly didn't really want to tell her mum about Paul. Everything seemed to upset Esther these days and they all tended to tiptoe a little around her. 'Well, Kay's just not able to cover the department.'

'Your brother's going to be in Mongolia next year,' Esther said. 'I've got everyone coming…'

'I know all that,' Holly said. 'And I'll do all I can to be here but I had last Christmas and New Year off and we have to take turns. There are mums with little children and—'

'Holly, I'm a mother and I *want* my family together this Christmas. Surely, given the year we've all had, that's not too much to ask?'

'I don't do the off duty, Mum,' Holly pointed out, but she could see that her mother was upset. So too was Holly. It had been a difficult enough day, without having to justify that she was needed at work, but Esther wouldn't let it go.

'Holly, they can't just expect you to change your plans at the last minute…'

You do, Holly was tempted to point out, but she didn't want to row.

Actually, she did.

Once they had been able to bicker, once Holly had been able to have a proper conversation with her mum, and she missed those times. 'I'm going to take my bag upstairs.'

She did just that and back in her old bedroom Holly sat for a moment on her old bed and took in a deep breath.

Pollyanna indeed!

She wanted to go back down and speak her mind, which was that she was tired of walking on eggshells around her mother.

Holly was, in fact, tired.

Not just from a late night and long drive but from a very difficult year. Right now she had problems of her own. Okay, not major ones, but she was wrestling with last night and wondering if she might never even see Daniel again, but there just wasn't a place for that now. Her mother had no idea what was going on in Holly's life and lately never thought to ask.

She looked up as there was a knock on the door and saw that it was her father. 'Your mum said that you might not be able to get Christmas off.'

'It looks that way.'

'Holly, I know they were good to last year but you know what Christmas means to your mum. Is there any way—?'

'Dad, the charge nurse who was supposed to be working over Christmas had her husband go into cardiac arrest in front of her last night.'

'Oh.'

'Yes, "oh". I want to be with my family at Christmas but so too does everyone else and Mum sending you up here to talk to me doesn't change that. Everyone's Christmas is important.'

Apart from the rather jumpy start it was a nice weekend. Holly went shopping with her mum and actually got rather a lot done, including ordering the turkey, but as pleasant as it had been, Holly arrived back at work more tired for her days off than when she had left.

There was no word from Daniel.

She hadn't expected flowers or a phone call, or a follow-up date.

But she *had* hoped.

And those hopes had been dashed.

What part of 'one-night stand' don't you get, Holly? she asked herself.

The 'one night' part.

How could something that had been so good simply end?

CHAPTER FIVE

HOLLY KNEW SHE shouldn't take her coffee back to bed.

It was five-thirty and she started work at seven so really she should be hitting the shower, but instead she allowed herself one small luxury that was becoming a habit of late.

Not just for Holly.

The whole emergency department were *thrilled* with their Advent calendars.

It was the fifteenth of December, which meant that so far fourteen chocolaty delights had been eaten.

They had ranged from raspberry to mulled wine, from salted caramel to sticky toffee, and each was a masterpiece.

Every morning the staff all compared their treat.

Holly found the window that said fifteen and peeled back the little door and there it was—a little ball of chocolate with red and green dotted through it and dusted in icing sugar, and with a flurry of relish she popped into her mouth.

It was awful!

So awful that despite three chews waiting for the taste sensation to hit she ended up spitting it out into a tissue. It was glacé cherries and this sickly-sweet chocolate. It was so bad that, had that been the first day's chocolate, none of the rest would have been opened and the calendar would have found its way straight to the bin.

Grumbling, removing the taste with a mug of coffee, Holly headed for the shower and then took the underground to work.

She caught sight of her reflection in the window and saw just how drab she looked, especially given that it was so close to Christmas.

It wasn't just her.

The department was rather gloomy.

Paul had at first rallied and been moved from Intensive Care to the coronary care unit, but just two days ago he had thrown off another clot and collapsed again. Now he was back on ICU on a ventilator.

It wasn't just that, though.

Now that Daniel wasn't around the days seemed longer and the run-up to Christmas, which Holly usually loved, felt just a little less, well, Christmassy.

Even the very thorough Kay was falling behind in her plans.

'Holly, can you sort out the Secret Santa?' Kay said as Holly took off her coat.

The underground had been packed, her boots had let in the rain and Holly's mood was a touch frazzled, possibly down to the fact she had her period, but she'd kill anyone who suggested it might be that.

'Nora usually does it…' Kay sighed.

'Sure,' Holly agreed.

'I'm going to have a cup of tea before we start.'

That sounded like a good idea to Holly.

'Hey,' Trevor said as Kay and Holly walked in with large mugs of tea. 'Did you have your chocolate this morning?'

Holly pulled a face and nodded.

'I still feel a bit sick,' Anna moaned.

'I think,' Holly said, 'that for the fifteenth one, the master chocolatier went on his break and left the work-experience kid in charge.'

They all laughed and then she startled because she recognised Daniel's. Turning, she saw that he was sitting behind where she stood. He was eating toast and drinking tea and Holly's heart told her to be wary.

This had the potential to really hurt!

'I thought you'd left,' Kay said.

'So did I,' Daniel admitted. 'But try telling that to Admin. They called me this morning at six and asked me to come in. I'm only here till midday, though.'

Holly ignored him.

It had been twelve days since she had last seen him.

The Twelve Days of Absence, Holly now named them, and if he expected her to be smiling and peppy and, oh, so pleased to see him then he was mistaken. Instead, she drank her tea as she sorted out the Secret Santa.

'What are you doing?' he asked Holly, who had taken a seat and written out a list and was now tearing it up.

'Secret Santa.' Holly said, but didn't look up, when usually she'd answer with a smile.

She didn't know how to be around Daniel. They'd been friends who flirted before, now they were...what?

Ex-lovers.

Or was that too grand a word to describe them?

Not for Holly.

She had no idea as to his feelings, if any, for her, no idea where she stood in the scheme of things.

Probably nowhere.

But Holly wanted to find out.

The morning flew by and all were kept busy, especially as Kay took herself off to the office to wrestle with the dreaded off duty. The Christmas roster was the most awaited one of the entire year. Kay had tried to put it off as Nora had assured her she'd be back, but with Paul's further deterioration it was now clear that wouldn't be the case.

To have to change it at the last minute was not a decision that Kay had taken lightly.

And to forge the Secret Santa was not something Holly took lightly either. She just had to know how Daniel felt.

She slipped into the changing room and wrote 'Holly Jacobs', 'Holly Jacobs', 'Holly Jacobs' out about twenty times and screwed them up into little balls.

The original names she took out and placed carefully in the pocket of her scrubs and then added the duplicate copies of her own name to the envelope. Then she went out and found him checking results on a computer as Kay held out a form for him to sign.

'Pick a name,' Holly said, and waved the envelope under his nose.

'I shan't be here for Christmas,' Daniel told her, 'so there's no point in taking one.'

'Everyone takes a name,' Holly said. 'It's all about getting into the Christmas spirit.'

Daniel rolled his navy eyes, which indicated what he thought of that, and got back to the computer screen.

'Take a name, Daniel,' Kay said. 'You can drop it off on your way to the airport if you don't work again. If you can't manage that then I always have extras given half the staff are off for Christmas. It's just a bit of fun.'

Daniel didn't do fun.

Well, he did, but it was a rather more sophisticated type of fun he indulged in.

Not stupid Christmas-present swaps where people sulked if they didn't get what they wanted or you forgot, but for the sake of peace he put in his hand and pulled out a name.

Holly Jacobs.

Of course it was.

He looked at her vivid green eyes and mop of dark curls that were, as always, coming loose.

'You're not allowed to say who you got,' Holly told him. 'Just stick within the price limit and put it under the tree. Usually we check when the name we have is working. So, say you had…' she plucked a name out of thin air '… Trevor, well, he finishes up on—'

'I get the drift,' Daniel interrupted.

'Good.'

Daniel got up from his stool and stalked off and Holly gave a little satisfied smile.

Now she'd finally know—if he got her something truly awful, or forgot completely, then she'd have to simply accept that he cared not a jot for her and it had just been a one-night stand. Maybe then she could turn off the fairy lights that were perpetually twinkling in her head when he was around.

'I'll take a name,' Kay said, and reached out her hand.

Oh!

For all her plotting and scheming, Holly hadn't thought of that. Kay was about to reach in and she had to come up with something fast.

Very fast! Because walking towards her was Anna, and she hadn't taken a name yet either.

Holly suddenly had visions of twenty gifts all with her name under the tree and it would look a bit suspicious, especially as she was the one organising the thing.

'Are you okay?' Kay checked, as Holly whipped the envelope away.

'No!' Holly said, and did the only thing she could think of.

She fled!

And one lie led to another, it truly did, because she had no choice but to dash off to the staff loos and close the door behind her.

'Holly…' Kay followed her in and stood on the other side of the door. 'What's wrong?'

'I just feel a bit…sick.' Oh, she was the worst liar but at least Kay couldn't see her blush as she quickly changed the names over. 'A bit dizzy.'

She finally came out and Kay looked at her with narrowed eyes.

'Do you need to go home?'

'No.'

'Thank goodness for that. Go and get a cup of tea and sit down.'

Oh, please don't be nice, Holly thought, but she did as she was told and took a seat back in the staffroom.

Daniel appeared ten minutes later.

'Kay said that you weren't feeling very well.'

'I'm fine.'

He grinned.

'What?'

'She's decided that you're pregnant.'

'Oh, God!' Holly groaned.

'You're not, are you?'

Daniel's grin had, she noted, disappeared.

'No.'

'You're sure? I mean, I know we were careful…'

'Shh…' Holly looked around to be sure there was no one near. 'There's nothing to worry about.'

'Well, if there was something to worry about…'

'There isn't.'

There wasn't.

'I've got my period.'

'Is that why you're in such a filthy mood?' Daniel asked.

'Nope, that would be the company,' Holly said. 'Don't worry, Daniel, there are no repercussions for you to worry about!' Holly gave him a tight smile and got up from her chair. 'I'd better get back to work.'

Daniel stood as she brushed past him and he knew that Holly was wrong, there were repercussions from that night. Their friendship had changed. Gone was the easygoing banter and the little flirts and gone too was the lie that once they'd slept together he'd be over her, as was usually the case.

Oh, he could blame it on being half-asleep that he'd said yes when Admin had rung this morning to ask him to work, but it was more than that. And he could insist to himself that he was still in England because he had found out that neither his father nor Amelia could make Maddie's nativity play this afternoon and so had decided to stick around for that.

He took out the bunched-up piece of paper from his pocket and read her name.

Holly Jacobs.

Yes, there were repercussions.

CHAPTER SIX

INDEED, KAY HAD pegged Holly as pregnant!

Before Holly could even make it back to the department, Kay had called her into the office for a little talk.

'I've worked with a lot of young women in my time and generally when they're dizzy and throwing up...' She went into her pocket and pulled out a pregnancy test. 'It's better to face things.'

'Kay, please.'

'You can talk to me, Holly...'

'I know that I can,' Holly said. 'But I'm not pregnant.'

As Kay held out the test, Holly refused to take it.

'You're not yourself, Holly!'

'Kay, I've got my period...'

'Well, it's the mother of a period, then, because it's lasted for two weeks. You've been awful,' Kay said, and Holly gave a reluctant smile. 'You can talk to me.'

Holly looked at Kay and she was touched by Kay's forthrightness and concern and, yes, she could talk to her. In some ways it would be a relief to tell someone how jumbled up she was feeling. Once she had been able to talk to her mother but those days seemed a long way off right now.

And so she told Kay the truth, well, a small part of it. 'I didn't feel sick or faint. I just had to come up with something. I didn't want you and Anna to take a name because I fudged the Secret Santa.'

'You what?' Kay frowned.

'It was only my name written down,' Holly explained.

'So that Daniel would choose you?' Kay said, smiling as realisation dawned. 'That's very ingenious. We'll have to see what he gets you.'

'Nothing, I expect.' Holly shrugged and Kay saw the sparkle of tears in her eyes.

'I don't think Daniel's very into Christmas.'

And Holly didn't think Daniel was very into her either.

'He's leaving, Holly,' Kay pointed out. 'He's made it very clear that he'll soon be off.'

Holly nodded. 'I wish he'd gone already.'

'No, you don't.'

Kay was right. This morning when she'd seen him, though cross and confused, she'd felt her heart simply leap at the sight of him. And now she had to start back at the beginning of getting over him when the last days had been hell.

She didn't just like Daniel, it felt like a whole lot more.

More than she'd ever liked anyone in her entire life.

Oh, she was trying so hard not to use the love word, even to herself.

Surely it couldn't be that?

'Be careful,' Kay suggested, and Holly nodded, even if it was a bit late for that. 'Now,' Kay added, 'while I can be terribly indiscreet I don't break confidences, so you don't have to worry about that. Daniel's lovely to chat to but I know his type—all he wants is inside your knickers, not your mind.' She saw Holly's pinched face and while she was delivering gloomy verdicts she decided to just get it over with. 'I've finished the Christmas roster. I'd better put it up.'

Holly knew that her cheeks had turned pink.

'Do you want a sneak preview?' Kay asked, and when Holly nodded she turned the computer screen around and Holly took a look.

She had been given a half-day on Christmas Eve, which meant that she finished at midday and was due back for a night shift on Christmas night, though she was off for New Year's Eve.

'I did my best,' Kay said.

Kay really had done, because at least there was a chance for Holly to make it home and spend the best part of Christmas with her family. Certainly Kay hadn't been gentle on herself—she was working all of it, just as she had last year and the year before that.

'Don't you ever want Christmas off?' Holly asked.

'Not really. Eamon used to get weary of me working it every year,' Kay admitted, 'but he's got used to it now. Next year I'm taking it off, though.'

She smiled that gorgeous Irish smile and Holly smiled back.

Kay's daughter, Louise, was due to give birth in the new year and Kay would be a first-time grandmother.

'I'm not missing that baby's first Christmas for the world,' Kay said as they walked through to the department.

The off duty had been posted and Holly stood back, chatting with Kay, as all the staff clustered around the computers.

'Louise might have the baby on Christmas Day,' Holly commented.

'God, I hope not,' Kay said, 'for the baby's sake. They never get a real birthday...'

'Yes, they do,' Holly said, and would have argued more

strongly but she suddenly remembered the Christmas that everyone in her immediate family would rather forget.

Because they'd forgotten her birthday.

Why today did everything make her want to cry?

'Holly!'

She looked over and saw that a patient was being wheeled in by Karen, a cheery paramedic.

The lady looked to be in her seventies and was very well dressed in a lovely woollen coat and scarf but she was sitting in the wheelchair, holding her arm, which was wrapped in a sling.

'This is Iris Morrison…'

It was a familiar injury at this time of the year. People were busy and the streets were slippery and when Iris had fallen she had put out her hand to save herself and had, it appeared, broken her wrist.

She was taken into a cubicle and Holly had a look at the wrist. It was causing Iris a lot of pain and she was also very pale, which meant Holly didn't really want her sitting for ages in a chair, so she decided to put her on a trolley.

The handover was brief. Iris was fit and well and was more cross with herself than anything.

'I haven't got time for a broken wrist,' she sighed when the paramedics had left.

'I think you're going to have to make time.' Holly smiled. It was terribly warm in the department and Iris's coat would have to come off for the X-ray, but Holly decided to do that after Iris had been given something for pain.

She told Iris she would be back in a moment and saw Daniel looking at *another* wrist X-ray.

'I've got a seventy-two-year-old lady…'

'I saw,' Daniel said.

'Can she have something for pain before I undress her?'

He nodded and took the patient card from Holly and then followed her in.

'Good morning, Mrs Morrison, I'm Dr Chandler.'

'Chandler?' Iris frowned and then looked up at navy eyes. 'I used to work for a Marcus Chandler, I'm guessing from those eyes that you must be Daniel!'

'That's correct.' Daniel gave her a smile. 'I'm sorry, I don't…'

'You were about five years old,' Iris said, 'so I don't expect you to remember. We've never actually met. I was your father's secretary for a year. He was a very impressive surgeon.'

'And you're a very tactful woman,' Daniel said, because his father was a very difficult man and he doubted any secretary of his had many nice words to say about him.

Iris laughed but then winced as Daniel gently examined her wrist. 'You don't need me to tell you it's broken?'

'No.'

'I'll get you something for the pain and then we'll get that coat off and get you straight round—'

'Actually,' Holly said, 'there's rather a wait for X-Ray.'

'I'll see if I can get you squeezed in,' Daniel said to Iris, and she gave a delighted smile at the upgrade.

Soon the coat was off and because of the strong pain-killers she had been given, Holly went to X-Ray with her.

Of course he had managed to squeeze Iris in because, from the way the radiographer was batting her eyelashes, she was another fan of Daniel's.

The entire female population was, it would seem.

'Gorgeous-looking young man, isn't he?' Iris smiled as they waited.

'He knows it,' Holly said.

'Well, he seems nice with it, though, not like his father. Oh, that man!' She rolled her eyes to indicate just how difficult Daniel's father had been. 'Such a fantastic surgeon but he was the coldest man I have ever come across. I tried to be nice, given that his wife had died, I mean I guessed it must be hard to be left with a five-year-old...'

Holly swallowed.

The thought of losing her mother had rocked Holly's world for more than a year and she was twenty-eight. Holly just sat there for a moment and tried to imagine a world without her mother in it from the age of five.

She couldn't.

And neither could Daniel imagine a world with a happy family in it.

They sort of danced around each other for the best part of the morning. Iris got a plaster on her wrist and was picked up by her daughter. Holly got caught up with a patient who needed to be closely watched as they waited for him to be admitted to the psychiatric unit.

At midday Daniel came out of the changing room to head for home and saw Holly sitting by the patient's trolley. She was reading a magazine while the patient slept.

'Still no bed for him?' Daniel checked.

'Another hour.'

She barely glanced up and Daniel, who was always so certain where woman were concerned, was less so now.

He didn't know what he wanted, and even if he did, he wasn't sure that an offer to catch up would be welcomed by Holly.

She didn't look happy, when Holly always had, and Daniel was sure he had contributed to that.

'Daniel?' Kay was walking past. 'I've just been speaking with Mr Edwards and he said to ask you if there's any chance you could stay on till five.'

'Sorry.' Daniel shook his head. 'I've already got plans.'

'What plans?' Kay busied herself with his business. 'A date?'

'You could say that,' Daniel answered without thinking, as Holly did all she could to stop her top lip from curling like the family Labrador's when someone reached for his bone.

'Have a nice Christmas, Holly,' Daniel said.

'I shall.'

She would!

Holly had spent way too long daydreaming about him.

When her shift ended and Holly raced to the department store where she'd been with Daniel a few weeks before, she found herself watching the glassblower for a little while.

Thanks to her own meddling, she had Daniel to buy a gift for.

Yes, while she would have loved to queue up and buy him a hand-blown Christmas decoration and have the elves write a letter, she had no idea what she'd have them write.

And it was far too expensive.

And it would be embarrassing to reveal just how much he meant to her.

Anyway, he probably wouldn't be back to claim his Secret Santa present, let alone deposit hers.

And so instead of pouring her heart out in a tiny letter that would never be read she headed to the men's floor and tried to decide on a more appropriate present for him.

Yes, she exceeded the strict Secret Santa budget, but not by a ridiculous amount. Holly bought him a lip balm for when he went skiing. It was a very nice lip balm, in fact, and as close to his lips as she'd allow herself to get again.

It was a nice little gift—personal but not too personal, and useful as well.

It wasn't a gift from the heart—Daniel had made it very clear that her heart was something he didn't want.

CHAPTER SEVEN

DANIEL HEADED STRAIGHT from work to Maddie's school but his mind was on Holly.

She was nothing like his usual type yet he had liked her on sight and that feeling had not just remained, it had grown.

The more he knew her the more he wanted to know, and for someone who did his best not to get too involved it was the oddest feeling.

It was also a very new feeling and one he'd done his best not to properly examine.

He knew that she liked him. And that wasn't arrogance speaking, that was concern. After all, Daniel knew his own reputation.

Then he got out of the car and knew that it was time to focus on Maddie. He was cross with both his father and Amelia for not being here today.

His mother had always made the effort to be there for stuff like that, Daniel thought, and as he did so he suddenly halted.

All these years later memories seemed to be coming in and he felt floored anew by each and every one of them. As he took his seat in the audience he remembered standing on a stage with a towel on his head and his father's tie, and looking out and seeing his mother nod and smile to him.

And so he did the same for Maddie as she came out.

She was dressed as an angel and had a silver tinsel halo and didn't stay in character at all because she smiled and waved to him when she was supposed to be being serious.

Daniel smiled and waved back.

It was actually rather good!

Joseph's front teeth were missing and there was a worrying moment when he nearly dropped baby Jesus and he and Maddie shared a little *yikes* look but apart from that it went well.

'Which one's yours?' a woman beside him asked and nodded towards the stage.

'The loud angel,' Daniel answered, so glad with his decision to delay his trip just so that Maddie could have a family member in the crowd.

Afterwards, in the playground, she ran to him.

'You were fantastic!' Daniel told her.

'I know.' Maddie beamed. 'Did you see when Thomas nearly dropped the baby?'

'I did.'

'Where are we going?' she asked with all the confidence of a sister who knew she would be getting an extra treat from her brother.

'I thought we might go to the movies.'

'Really?'

'Yes.' He told her what they would be seeing but instead of her eyes lighting up they were suddenly worried.

'I wanted to dress up when I saw that!'

'I thought that you might,' Daniel said, and handed her a bag he had brought with him. It was her princess costume that he had picked up from Jessica, the nanny, on his way back from work.

He waited as Maddie dashed off to the facilities and came out a few minutes later in all her finery and wearing a tiara, with her friends all oohing and ahhing as she paraded about.

'I love it when you pick me up from school.' Maddie said as he took out the booster seat from the boot of his car.

'I enjoy it too.'

He did.

'Why don't you do it more often?' Maddie asked as she jumped onto the booster seat, which Jessica had also given him, and strapped herself in.

Daniel didn't answer.

It wasn't picking Maddie up from school that was the problem, it was dropping her off and avoiding being asked in.

Maddie didn't notice his silence. As they drove off she did the royal wave to her friends from the back of the car.

'If you marry a prince do you *definitely* become a princess?' Maddie asked.

'Not necessarily,' Daniel said. 'You might become a duchess or a countess...'

'What's the point, then?' Maddie sighed.

Oh, she was her mother's daughter, but, unlike Amelia, Maddie made him laugh.

She was so cute and had the same navy eyes as he had and, for a five-year-old, was very good company.

'How is school?' Daniel asked as he drove.

'I love it,' Maddie said. 'How is your work at the other hospital?'

'I love it too,' Daniel said.

He did.

He'd *liked* working at his old hospital. He had been through medical school there, had worked his way through the ranks and had a strong network of friends. Yet for some reason working at The Primary felt right.

It wasn't about Holly, he wasn't that shallow. It was maybe that at The Primary he wasn't Marcus Chandler's son. There were no expectations. If anything, given that he was a locum there was the expectation he'd need his hand held and then an element of surprise when he shone.

Back to focusing on Maddie!

Except, even as Daniel parked his car, he rather wished Holly was here, for he had no idea what to do. He knew this wasn't going to be a quiet evening at the movies but there was an endless stream of little girls all dressed the same as Maddie and the queue for tickets was incredibly long.

For a moment he considered taking out his phone and booking on line—the nice seats where you had food brought to you—but he knew that wasn't the treat his little sister needed. Instead, they chatted with several other families as they waited to buy their tickets.

'How old is she?' a woman asked.

'Five.'

'Are you giving her mum a rest?'

Daniel gave a noncommittal nod—it was clear that again the woman thought that Maddie was his child and he certainly wasn't about to enlighten a stranger, or tell her that giving Amelia a rest was far from being the reason he was here.

'Is it nice to be out with your dad?' The woman smiled at Maddie.

'I don't get to go out with my dad very often!' Maddie pouted and the woman gave Daniel a cool stare and then turned away, no doubt assuming it was an access visit.

'Maddie,' he warned.

'Well, it's true. Me and Daddy hardly ever go out, he's always working. And when we do...' She blew out a breath that sent her fringe flying into her tiara. 'I hate it when he takes me to his club, it's so boring.'

Daniel said nothing but he thought of the long afternoons he had spent at that bloody club, sitting with a colouring book and pencils as the adults carried on outside.

He had hated it too.

Still, they were a world away from a stuffy club this afternoon. Instead, it was all about a bucket of popcorn and two large icy drinks and just a couple of hours checking out of the world.

The place was bedlam.

Children were cheering and singing along to the film.

One little boy was so overexcited and overfed that he vomited.

'Should you say you're a doctor?' Maddie checked.

'I don't think his mum needs a doctor to work out what's wrong.'

Maddie smiled and got back to enjoying the movie.

It was fun, it was light-hearted and it was exactly what big brother and little sister needed. All too soon though it was over and they were headed for home.

After a few hours of easy conversation as they sat in a line of traffic making its slow way out of the car park, suddenly Maddie was quiet.

'Are you tired?' Daniel asked looking in the rear-view mirror, where she stared ahead.

'No,' Maddie answered. And then, as only five-year-olds could, she asked a question. 'Why aren't you going to be there at Christmas?'

Daniel took a moment to answer. 'I'm going away on a trip, it's been planned for a long time.'

'But it's only ten more sleeps until Christmas...'

'Maddie!' His tone told her to be quiet and he sounded like his father so he changed tack. 'I don't know exactly when I'm leaving.'

But it wasn't just Christmas that was troubling her. 'I don't want you to go.'

She broke into noisy sobs and Daniel stared ahead, not really knowing how he felt himself, let alone what to say. He could point out that it was just for a year. But a year was for ever when you were five years old.

He wasn't about to change his plans because his little sister kicked up. He was thirty-two, for God's sake, he was hardly going to stick around because his father had decided to attempt to parent...

Only it wasn't about his father.

'I hardly see you any more,' Maddie said.

'We've been out tonight,' Daniel pointed out.

'Only because you're saying goodbye. I don't see you so much any more.'

Daniel hadn't seen much of Maddie for the first couple of years of her life.

He and his father had barely been speaking when Maddie had been born. Daniel didn't really approve of his father taking such a very young bride. In turn his father was furious that Daniel had decided he didn't want to be a surgeon. When Maddison had been born, he had been pretty much told to stay back and that Amelia and Maddison were his father's family now.

At first it had suited him fine. Daniel wasn't exactly into babies and he'd just dropped off a birthday present or stood at the christening and things. But then Maddison the baby had become Maddie the two-year-old, with a smile and a cheeky personality that had soon endeared her to him.

And she was his family now.

Daniel didn't want to be some distant figure so he had started to factor her more into his life.

Till last Christmas when Amelia had come on to him.

Daniel's intention had been to be as far away as humanly possible this Christmas, to just stay out of his father's life, only it wasn't proving that easy.

'Look,' he said as the car pulled up at the picture-perfect house. 'I don't know what my plans are yet. I've got a lot of things going on now, Maddie. Grown-up stuff.'

'I hate grown-up stuff.'

'So do I.'

He really did.

'Please can I see you for Christmas?'

Daniel wanted to be able to just say no. To go home and hop on the internet and choose a flight and hotel. He looked over at what had once been his family home and though there were few happy memories of his time there, it didn't have to be that way for Maddie.

No, he would not stay for long but, yes, he could drop in and make a five-year-old happy on Christmas Day.

'I'll come around on Christmas Day to bring your present.'

Maddie gave a little squeal and smile and then climbed down from her seat, which Daniel collected, along with her school uniform.

Jessica came to the door and Daniel explained they'd had a good time, but that Maddie had just got a bit teary on the way home.

'She doesn't want you to leave.' Jessica nodded.

'Well, I'll be there for a little while on Christmas Day.'

Jessica opened her mouth to say something and then changed her mind and just gave him a smile. 'That's good,' she said.

Both knew that he was just delaying the inevitable—Maddie was going to be very upset when it really came time for him to leave.

His phone buzzed as he got back into the car and it was the agency he had signed up with, offering him various shifts. He was about to decline and point out that he had finished up.

Yet, given to what he'd agreed to for Maddie, he was here for at least another week.

'Are you available to work Christmas Eve, nine a.m. until till four p.m., in Outpatients at The Primary Hospital?'

'No,' Daniel said.

'Well, there's a night shift on New Year's Eve at the Royal.'

'No, thank you!' His response was a little sarcastic. There was no way that he'd work a night on New Year's Eve, and especially not at the Royal, he had seen in way too many there. He was about to explain that he was no longer available when she offered him one more shift.

'Well, you can't blame me for trying. What about Christmas Eve in Emergency at The Primary?'

And maybe this shift was the one he had been holding out for and perhaps the reason he hadn't taken himself completely off the books.

'What time?' Daniel asked.

'Seven a.m. until four.'

Holly would be on that morning, Daniel knew.

But even though she sprang to mind first, it wasn't just Holly that drew him back to The Primary. He liked the department and vibe there. He thought of Mr Edwards and Kay who had come to see him a valued part of the team, and he wanted to know how Nora's husband was going.

There were worse places to spend Christmas Eve, Daniel reasoned.

One more shift and he could find out all that had been going on and see how Holly was doing and hopefully he could manage a much better goodbye than the tense, stilted farewell they had achieved today.

'I'll take it,' Daniel agreed.

And so, if he was to be working on Christmas Eve, it meant that he needed to shop and so on the Saturday before Christmas, possibly the busiest shopping day of the year, he found himself back in the department store he had been to with Holly.

If he was going to stick to the Secret Santa budget then here really wasn't the place.

Except he knew what to get Holly, and so Daniel spent three very long hours thinking of what to put in a tiny letter.

But where to start?

Given he was standing here weeks after the event, yes, it had been more than a one-night stand.

And yet he was leaving.

It was getting harder and harder to do that.

There was family, namely Maddie, who needed him, a potential consultant's position at The Primary, which he was coming to love.

And there was Holly.

Yet there was so much more that he needed to sort out. His whole life had been spent failing to live up to his father's expectations, and falling off the chosen path.

Daniel knew he needed to sort out what it was that he wanted, and to do that he needed to get away.

'Your turn.'

Daniel looked down at a very harried and angry-looking lady dressed as an elf.

'What do you want written?'

'I haven't…' Daniel could feel the impatience in the people behind him. It had been more than a three-hour wait and he hadn't yet made up his mind.

And then he decided and took a little seat and told the lady what he wanted to be written.

She started typing on her mini-keyboard.

'That's it?' she checked.

'That's it,' Daniel agreed.

'Anything else?' she checked, clearly less than impressed with Daniel's attempt at expressing himself.

'No.'

'Well, I think you can do better than that.'

'I wasn't made aware that the letters got graded,' Daniel told her.

'The elves have all been trained—'

'Stop!' Daniel said. 'We both know you're not a real elf.'

She pursed her lips but after a brief standoff finally she hit 'send'.

'You can move down the line and watch your letter arrive.'

'Thank you.'

Daniel moved along the line and waited by the magic chute, scarcely able to believe he was doing this. He pressed cynical lips together as he thought of the computer and printer beneath the festive arrangement and then out it came—his letter to Holly.

He was asked to verify that it was indeed his letter and Daniel peered through a magnifying glass and read it.

Despite the fake elf's misgivings, Daniel worried that it actually said too much…but he nodded in agreement and then watched the glassblower work his magic.

It had cost a fortune.

It wasn't the money, or the time it took to make it, it was the fact that it was the closest he had come to sharing what was in his heart.

It was stay or go.

And staying felt harder.

CHAPTER EIGHT

CHRISTMAS EVE HAD always been special to Holly, whether or not she was working. The last-minute preparations, the excitement and anticipation and a certain sense of panic all seemed to combine to make it a truly magical day.

Last year, finding out that her mother was so unwell had had meant that it had been busy and fraught rather than exciting.

This year...

Holly looked around the bedroom and there was no sense of panic because everything was already done. Her presents were all wrapped and under the tree, last night she had gone and got petrol and now all she had to do was load up the car, drive to work, do her morning shift and wait for that once familiar, excited feeling to arrive.

Last night, for the first time, she had let herself cry properly over Daniel.

Determined to just let it all out so she didn't rot up everyone's Christmas, Holly had had a very good cry over a man who...

What?

She couldn't be angry because he had done nothing wrong. Daniel had been open and honest from the start. It was she who had taken it all too seriously and had kept looking for deeper meanings to everything. And so she had cried because she was simply sad that he was leaving.

Possibly he had already gone.

Half-heartedly she opened up number twenty-four on her Advent calendar and tried not to remember the time she and Daniel had done the same in this very bed.

It was a very nice-looking truffle, and when she bit into it there was a decadent shot of chocolate mousse.

Holly smiled because it was true—chocolate *always* helped.

A bit.

And there could be a chance that she would still see Daniel. Maybe he'd stop by with her Secret Santa present today, Holly thought, because there had been nothing under the tree at work last night.

And then she stopped.

Holly just stopped with hoping and wishing that things could be different between herself and Daniel and decided that she was being greedy and asking for too much. Last year, despite a rather dire diagnosis, she had prayed for a Christmas miracle and that her mother would still be here next year.

Esther was.

And so Holly got out of bed and showered and pushed all dark thoughts aside and refused to give her favourite time of the year over to a man who refused to embrace it or even bother to celebrate it.

Holly pulled on black jeans and boots and a red jumper for the commute to work. Her hair was particularly wild this morning but she just ran her fingers through the curls and decided to tie it back once she got to work. Red lipstick might be a bit much for the emergency department but it went with red earrings that flashed and she *refused* to be miserable today.

It was Christmas Eve after all!

Daniel wasn't in the least miserable.

He woke early and found that he was still looking forward to his shift at The Primary.

Breakfast was coffee, along with the most amazing chocolate truffle that he had ever tasted. Once showered and dressed he went and got Holly's present from the cupboard where it sat beside Maddie's and also presents for both his father and Amelia.

It was looking a little more like Christmas in his flat than it ever usually did.

But even if he was in a good mood Daniel spent the drive to work worrying that the present he had got for Holly was far too much and she might end up reading more into it than there was.

Still, he wanted her to have it, even if it just served as a nice memory of the wonderful night they had spent.

It had meant something.

She finished at midday, Daniel knew. That meant he could give it to her on her way out.

But even so…

He'd play it by ear, Daniel decided as he parked in the staff car park and got out. He had a small satchel that held his laptop and things and he placed the decoration carefully in there and went to make his way over to Emergency.

'Daniel!' The shout went up almost as soon as he'd got out of his car. He'd know that voice anywhere and he turned to see Kay frantically waving and standing next to Holly.

'We need a hand,' Kay called out to him in urgent tones.

'Okay.' He nodded.

'Hurry!' Kay called, and Daniel moved faster, wondering if someone had fainted or, from the way Kay was urging him, been run over, or...

'What?' he asked when he got there to find that nothing seemed amiss.

'I don't think Holly should leave all her family's presents in the car in case they're pinched, so if you could help us to carry them in...'

'I thought someone was hurt!' Daniel scolded.

'Why would you think that?' Kay asked as she handed him several Christmassy-looking bags that were all crammed to the brim with gifts. 'I just don't want to be late.'

He and Holly smiled and it was the first time that they had shared a proper smile since, well, since that night and the morning after.

Things had been awkward between them but felt a little less so today.

'How's Paul?' he asked as they started to walk.

'Don't ask.' Kay shook her head but Daniel wasn't going to be fobbed off.

'I just did!'

Holly answered for Kay. 'They're going to try and get him off the ventilator this morning. If not, he'll have to go to Theatre for a tracheostomy. He's been very up and down but mainly down.'

'It's been more than three weeks,' Kay sighed.

And both Holly and Daniel looked ahead because, yes, it had been a little more than three weeks since their night together also.

Hope was fading for all concerned.

'We'll put them in my office.' Kay suggested.

'Okay.' Holly nodded. 'I'll drop these off and then go back for the last lot.'

'There's more?' Daniel checked.

'Yep.'

'Give me those,' he said to Holly, unable to believe just how many presents she had. 'Go back and get the rest.'

Holly passed all her bags and parcels to him and Daniel staggered inside. Kay dropped the few she was carrying by her desk and then dashed off to grab a quick drink before handover, and Daniel realised that he suddenly had a chance to hide the decoration he had bought for the Secret Santa.

He went into his satchel and took out her gift.

It was too much, Daniel knew, and would cause loads of gossip if she opened it in front of everyone as she would surely know, straight away, that it was from him.

Yet he wanted her to have it and he wanted her to know how he felt.

But only once he had gone.

And now he could see the way to do just that, and so he slipped it into a bag that had a picture of a smiling snowman on it. So Holly! he thought as he headed for the staffroom.

'Did you bring your Secret Santa gift?' Kay checked, and Daniel pulled a face to indicate that he had forgotten.

'Oh, come on, Daniel,' Kay said. 'I'll see if I've got something you can put out.'

There was time for only a very quick drink but they all took it.

'Morning,' Trevor said, placing a beautifully wrapped present under the fake Christmas tree in the staffroom.

'And a delicious, delicate chocolate mousse truffle morning it is,' Kay said, and everyone laughed.

Daniel included.

They actually made him laugh, Daniel thought.

They found the happy in the smallest things and then watered it till it grew.

'That Advent calendar should be illegal.' Daniel joined in the conversation. 'I've been to three discount stores now but they've all sold out.' He looked up to see that Holly had come in.

'We're all worried,' she said.

'Worried? About what?'

'That the same work-experience student that made the ones on the fifteenth was let loose again and that the big day shall disappoint.'

'It never disappoints,' Kay said.

Holly, as she glanced under the Christmas tree and saw that Daniel hadn't added to the pile, rather thought that this year it might!

'So this is your last shift?' Kay asked Daniel as they all headed into the kitchen to drop off their mugs before their shift started. 'He's like that rock star…what's-his-name?'

'I have no idea,' Holly muttered as she rinsed her mug.

'The one who keeps doing his sell-out farewell tour and then a year later comes back and does it all over again.'

Kay allocated the staff and Holly was to work in the main section, which was where Daniel would mainly be, unless he had to go into Resus.

Holly was conflicted.

Though she had thought she wanted to see him, now that he was here it was proving hard.

Happy!

Holly kept reminding herself that it was Christmas Eve and that soon she'd be on the much-awaited and hard fought-for drive home!

Yay!

The patient who had just arrived, though, looked as grumpy as she felt.

'Leave me alone,' he told the paramedics as he was moved over onto the trolley. 'I don't want to be here!'

Holly had already gathered that.

Albert—he refused to give his surname or his date of birth—was homeless and had been found collapsed in a doorway. It was unclear how long he had been unconscious. The paramedics explained that the shopkeeper who had called for an ambulance had said he was used to him being there when he closed up at night.

He was usually awake by morning and told to move on.

They just hadn't been able to wake him this morning but he had sat up when the paramedics had arrived and insisted that he was fine. Albert had tried to get up and walk off but had been unable to do so and had finally agreed to come to hospital and be seen.

He was cantankerous, and very, very unkempt, with wild white hair and sore, cracked skin, and he refused to get undressed. More worrying than his appearance was a deep cough and a tinge of purple to his lips and tongue.

Holly checked his oxygen saturation, which was rather low so she slipped on some nasal prongs to deliver a low dose of oxygen as she took his temperature.

'You've got a fever.'

He nodded.

'Let me help get you into a gown so that the doctor can examine you.'

'I don't want you cutting my clothes.' He was coughing and wheezing but finally he allowed Holly to start removing layer upon layer of clothes.

First a coat, then a jumper, beneath that a jacket and then another shirt.

Kay came in and helped with his boots and bottom half.

It was always a bit of a feat to undress the homeless, especially in winter.

Soon, though, it was all bagged into two large plastic bags that Holly put under his trolley. Albert held onto a small leather bag and refused when Holly offered to lock it up in the hospital safe for him.

'You're not touching this!'

So Holly didn't.

And neither did she get very far with all the questions that needed to be asked and forms that needed to be filled in. He didn't want to reveal even his surname, let alone his next of kin.

'Is there anyone I can let know you are here?' Holly asked.

He gave a derisive laugh.

'Do you have any medical history that we need to know about?'

Albert didn't answer, and neither did he let Holly put in an IV or take bloods. All he wanted to do was to be left alone to sleep. Soon enough Daniel came into examine him.

Albert was more responsive to Daniel's questions than he had been to Holly's and he did let him listen to his chest.

'How long have you had this cough for?'

'It's been bad for a couple of days.'

'You've got quite a high temperature,' Daniel commented, and Albert nodded.

'I've had that since last night,' Albert said. 'I got the

shakes and I couldn't get warm but I think I was burning up.'

'Okay,' Daniel said, and he helped him lie back on the pillows and had a feel of his stomach, and though he tried to talk to him Albert didn't really communicate.

'I'm going to take some blood and then get an IV started,' Daniel said. 'We'll get a chest X-ray...' He went through it all but Albert just lay back. 'You can have some breakfast while you're waiting to go around, it's a bit of a wait.'

'I don't want breakfast.'

'Well, a cup of tea...'

'I don't want anything.'

Daniel could see that he was markedly dehydrated. The IV he was putting in would take care of that but he was more concerned with his lethargy.

'Is there anything else going on, Albert?'

'Everything's fine!' Albert's response was sarcastic and Holly watched as instead of leaving Daniel remained.

'How long have you been on the streets?'

'Long enough,' Albert said, but then he opened up a little. He had lived rough, on and off, for eighteen years. 'Sometimes I stay at a hostel and I was at a halfway house once for a few weeks but it didn't work out.'

He relied on several charities and soup kitchens for some meals and had to beg for help with the rest and he didn't want to see a social worker.

'I just want my chest sorted out and then I'll be gone.'

'How old are you, Albert?' Daniel asked, and though he had refused to answer Holly, now he did.

'Seventy-two.'

'And winter's barely got going,' Daniel said, and Holly saw Albert close his eyes at the thought of the prospect of another winter living rough but then he rallied and gave a shrug.

'It's not so bad.'

'Really?' Daniel checked, but Albert didn't answer. He just lay on his back and stared up at the ceiling as Daniel took some bloods and an IV was commenced.

'Would you like some breakfast?' Holly offered again once Daniel had gone, but again Albert shook his head.

'Leave me alone.'

The wait for X-Ray was a long one but finally he was back in the unit and sure enough he had lower lobe pneumonia along with a few more chronic issues.

He was started on antibiotics and as Holly added them to his IV she tried to engage him.

Albert was having none of it.

'I'm going to call the kitchen and see if they can send you something hot to eat,' Holly said, removing the untouched sandwiches that she had put out for him. 'I'll be back soon to do your obs.'

Daniel came in just as Holly left.

'She's a chirpy little thing, isn't she?' Albert grumbled.

'You could say that,' Daniel agreed. 'The admitting doctors will be down to see you, though it may be a while, but you're going to need to stay in.'

Often patients like Albert declined admission or set a very strict timeline for treatment, such as a few hours, but Albert nodded.

If anything, he seemed relieved that he would be staying in.

'How are you doing?' Daniel asked.

'Still coughing.'

'You shall be for a while,' Daniel said. 'I meant, apart from your chest?'

'I'm just...' Daniel waited patiently and finally Albert elaborated. 'I'm tired.'

It was as if everything was summed up in that short statement and Daniel knew he was hearing the very truth.

Tired of being sick.

Tired of a hard life on the streets.

And now that he had admitted just how tired he was it was almost as if he had given up because he lay back defeated.

'Albert, while you're waiting to be seen, I'm going to call the duty social worker.'

'What's she going to do?'

'Perhaps she can get the ball rolling on some accommodation for when you're discharged.'

'I'm not going to another of those hostels. There are too many rules.'

'Albert, why won't you let us help you?'

'Because I don't want your help.'

Daniel wasn't so sure that was true.

'So do you want me to ring the social worker?' he checked.

'Call her if you want to.' Albert shrugged. 'I don't know what she's going to be able to do, though.'

Daniel called the duty social worker from the nurses' station, where the radio was playing Christmas carols and there was a plate of star-shaped gingerbread out. Most of the nurses were now wearing tinsel, but for Daniel it all felt a long way from Christmas.

Actually, it felt like every Christmas he had known.

'Nora!' Daniel looked up as a flushed-faced Nora came in.

'I'm looking for Kay,' she said, and then promptly burst into tears.

He paged Kay, who was dealing with a domestic violence incident, and led a teary Nora around to Kay's office.

'Nora...' Kay rushed in.

'He's talking!' Nora said through her tears. 'He knows where he is and everything.'

Daniel blinked.

He had been absolutely sure that Paul must have died and from Kay's gaping mouth she must have been thinking the same. But it would seem instead that Nora had been holding things in all these weeks and now that the news was good she could finally allow some of her emotions out.

'They're thrilled with him,' she sobbed.

Daniel left them to it.

Who would have thought?

Not he.

He walked past the cubicle and there was Albert, just lying there dozing, but he opened his eyes as Daniel approached.

'I spoke with the social worker. Now that she knows you're being admitted—'

'She'll see me on the ward.' Albert knew the drill and finished Daniel's sentence for him.

Daniel nodded. With public holidays and a very heavy workload at this time of the year, they both knew it might take a while for Albert to be seen.

'You'll be here over Christmas,' Daniel told him. 'Is there anyone you'd like us to inform?'

'I doubt they'd want to know.'

It was an opening and the first hint of the life that Albert had left behind.

'Have you ever been in touch with your family?'

'No.' Albert shook his head. 'Well, I used to send a card to Emily, my great-niece, she's also my god-daughter, but

I wasn't well one year and I didn't manage to post it, then it seemed too late by the next.'

Daniel could see how it had happened. Oh, their lives were different in many ways but he could easily see how a couple of years of no contact might then make it hard to get back in touch.

And to know if you would even be welcome if you did.

'How old is she?' Daniel asked.

'Emily?' Albert checked, and Daniel nodded. 'She was two the last time I saw her. She'd be twenty now, I doubt she'd even know my name.'

'What about her parents?'

'Dianne is her mother,' Albert explained. 'She was my late sister's daughter. She's a chirpy thing too, like your young nurse. Dianne was good to me. Everyone took sides during the divorce but she always stayed back from doing that. I wasn't well.' He tapped the side of his head to indicate mental-health issues. 'Dianne always invited me over for Christmas but I'd always mess it up and start a row.'

'Why?'

'So that I could leave,' Albert admitted. 'I was embarrassed. I used to be a geography teacher. I missed out on head of department…they said I wasn't up to the responsibility but instead of proving them wrong, I proved them right and walked out. My wife had had enough by then and, looking back, I can't blame her. I lost my marriage, my job, everything really…' He shook his head. 'It's history.'

'I thought you said you taught geography.'

The silly joke made Albert smile but then Daniel watched as a very independent but very lonely man gave in then and started to cry.

It was very sad to watch but Daniel did so, and pulled

out some paper hand cloths from the dispenser so that Albert could blow his nose.

Holly came in to the sound of his tears but saw that Daniel was in there and left.

'Have you ever spoken with your wife?' Daniel asked when Albert had finished.

'I was admitted to hospital once when the divorce wasn't yet through,' Albert said. 'They called her but she told them that she wanted nothing more to do with me. I can't blame her for that.'

Daniel knew that the social worker would go through it all with Albert but that could be a few days away and, Daniel guessed, by then Albert could well have taken up his things and gone.

'Have you thought of calling your niece?' Daniel asked.

'Every day,' Albert admitted, and he went into the small bag that he would not let go of and took out a clear plastic bag. On it was a piece of paper and in very neat handwriting there was a number and his niece's full name and address. 'I don't know what to say if I call.'

Neither did Daniel.

Nearly two decades on, what did you say?

'They might have moved...' Daniel said as he looked at the address, but Albert shook his head.

'They're still there,' Albert said.

'How do you know?'

'Sometimes I walk past. There's a "For Sale" sign up, though. They shan't be there for long.'

It was now or never.

'Do you want me to try and call for you?' Daniel offered.

He rather hoped that Albert would shake his head. Daniel really did, because he didn't want to walk back into the cubicle and have to tell Albert that his family had terminated the call, as often happened in situations like these.

There was a lot of hurt on both sides, no doubt.

But instead Albert nodded. 'I'd like that,' he said. 'Please.'

Daniel took a few more details and as he walked out, Holly was walking toward him, carrying a tray. Her hair was piled up high and her smile was bright, if a bit forced, when she saw him. 'I got the canteen to send Albert up an early lunch.'

'Good,' Daniel said. 'I'm just about to call his niece, they haven't been in touch for eighteen years. I think Albert's hoping to resume contact.'

He watched as her smile faded. Holly would know only too well that the chances of this call ending well weren't great.

Daniel held the cubicle curtain open for Holly and she walked in with the tray. 'I've got a nice potato and leek soup for you, Albert, and it actually smells rather amazing.'

'You have it, then.'

Holly arranged the tray on a table and pushed it towards him but Albert wasn't interested. Instead, he lay back on the pillows and closed his eyes and wondered what the doctor would say when he returned.

Daniel wasn't hopeful.

He dialled the number that Albert had given him. It had been many years and given the little history Albert had told him Daniel wasn't sure that he'd be speaking to the right person, let alone that the call would be welcome, or that anyone would even pick up.

Someone did. 'Hi!'

'Hello,' Daniel responded to the cheery voice. 'I was wondering if I could speak with Dianne Eames.'

'She's not here at the moment.' The voice was that of a young woman and she sounded busy. 'Who's calling?'

'It's Dr Daniel Chandler from the accident and emergency department at The Primary Hospital.'

That tended to get a response!

'One moment...' She must have covered the phone but Daniel heard the young woman call for her mother and a few moments later another woman came to the phone.

'Dianne Eames speaking.'

She sounded brusque and impatient but, Daniel knew, that was often the way to cover fear.

'Is everything okay with Vince?' she asked.

'We had a patient admitted to us this morning. Albert Marlesford...'

There was a long stretch of silence.

'How is he?'

Daniel had to think for a moment before answering. 'He's been admitted with pneumonia. But, I'm not sure if you're aware, he's been living on the streets for some time.'

'Yes, I'm more than aware. That was his choice.'

'I understand that.'

'We tried to keep in touch with him, he used to send the odd card or letter and I'd go out looking for him...' There was a tense, inward breath that was followed by the sound of tears. 'He always managed to mess up Christmas every year, you could guarantee it!'

Given that it was Christmas Eve, Daniel thought for a moment that the message was clear—Albert wouldn't be messing up this one—but it would seem he had misinterpreted, Daniel realised, as Dianne continued to speak.

'Now he's managed another. I guess there won't be turkey at the table tomorrow.'

'Sorry?'

'I was just on my way to pick it up but that can wait… He's at The Primary, you say…'

It was then that Daniel realised that Dianne was saying that she was on her way in. That, even after eighteen years of no contact, Albert's niece would drop everything, even plans for tomorrow's dinner, to come and see him on Christmas Eve.

'Dianne,' Daniel said. 'To be honest, I think by the time you've got your turkey he might be a little more ready to receive visitors.' He decided it might be better for Albert if he explained things now. 'It might be nicer for him to be a bit more presentable when you meet.'

'He was always too proud for his own good,' Dianne said, and then thought for a moment. 'Can you tell him that I'll be in to see him this afternoon…? Hold on a moment.' Daniel waited and there was the sound of chatter in the background. 'Can you let him know that Emily will be in to see him too?'

She gave Daniel her mobile number and asked that she be called immediately if there was any change.

And that was it.

The phone call ended but instead of going immediately to tell Albert, Daniel sat for a long moment staring at the phone.

He had expected a cool reception, even to have the phone hung up on him, or at best to be bombarded with questions. Dianne hadn't required an immediate update on all the missing years, all she had needed to know was where Albert was, to be there for him.

Daniel walked over to his cubicle and saw that Holly was still in there, trying to persuade him to at least try and have a little something to eat, but Albert ignored her and simply closed his eyes.

'I just spoke with Dianne,' Daniel said, and he saw that Albert's eyes remained closed, no doubt bracing himself for rejection. 'She's going to come in a bit later with Emily.'

Then Albert's eyes opened.

'She said that?' Albert checked, and Daniel nodded and he watched as Albert's face broke into a smile.

'She was just on her way to pick up the turkey but she offered to come straight in...'

It was then that Albert started fretting. 'I can't see her looking like this....' How he looked was one of the many reasons that Albert hadn't knocked on his niece's door. 'I smell...'

'We can sort all that, Albert.' Holly spoke then. 'In fact, you get an early Christmas present!'

There was always stash of clothes in Emergency and Kay kept them in the same cupboard that she kept Christmas gifts. The clothes came mainly in the form of donations from staff and fundraisers and they were very valued, especially in situations such as this.

As well as clothes for Christmas, Kay ensured there were always presents, for the children, for the overnight patients, for people such as Albert, and she shopped throughout the year just for situations such as this.

Holly went into the dark storeroom and turned on the light. First she went through the men's clothes and found some smart navy pyjamas that looked large enough for Albert. They weren't new, but they were very neat, and the colour wasn't faded and all the buttons were on. Then she went through the wrapped gifts—they were separate barrels for men, women and children, and the gifts were also labelled by age.

On the shelf was a stash of chocolate stockings, already wrapped for anyone who might have been forgotten, but there were more pressing things than that needed for Albert today.

His early present was soap, deodorant and a comb.

As well as a wash Holly gave him a tidy-up shave with eyebrows and ears thrown in!

'Well, look at you!' Kay said as Holly prepared to move Albert up to the ward. 'You're looking grand.'

'I'm feeling it,' Albert said.

Okay, he was still rather rough around the edges and Kay looked at his feet, which were peeking out from the blanket. They would be attended to by the podiatrist at a later stage but for now he got an extra present of fluffy socks and he was certainly ready to meet his niece and great-niece again.

Holly smiled as she walked into the acute medical unit. It was far more elaborately decorated than Emergency—in fact, they had won the competition for Best Decorations.

Emergency hadn't even placed.

'Good morning, Albert,' a cheerful male nurse said. 'Actually, it's almost afternoon. You're just in time for lunch.'

'Good,' Albert huffed. 'I'm starving.'

'Have they been keeping you hungry down there?' The nurse smiled at Holly, who rolled her eyes. Her whole morning had been spent trying to get Albert to eat. 'We've put you in a four-bedded ward...' He gave directions to Holly. 'Bay Six.'

Bay Six had three other gentleman in it. Two were asleep but one nodded and said hello to Albert, who gave a cheery wave back.

'Thank you,' Albert said, once she had him settled in bed. 'Are you working over Christmas?'

'I'm just about to finish,' Holly said. 'Though I'll be back tomorrow night.'

'Well, thank you again.'

It was the nicest note to end her shift on. It was just so lovely to see Albert tucked up in bed and knowing that he'd be taken care of over Christmas. Holly made her way down to Emergency rather quickly. It was already after midday and she still had to get all her parcels out of Kay's office.

She would not be saying goodbye to Daniel, Holly had already decided. She had said it too many times, and on each occasion it hurt a little more. Anyway, he was busy with a patient and that suited Holly just fine. She loaded up the gifts and chatted to Kay, who was taking a quick break in her office.

'Have a wonderful Christmas, Holly,' Kay said. 'Now, don't go breaking your neck to get here by nine tomorrow night. I can stay back for an hour or so.'

'I should be fine.' Holly smiled. She had her presents piled up on a wheelchair and was ready to make a quick exit.

There was just one more thing, Kay reminded her.

'Did you get your present from under the tree?'

There hadn't been one there for her on her coffee break and Holly had tried to pretend that it didn't matter.

'Oh!' Holly feigned surprise, as if it was the furthest thing from her mind. 'I'll go now.'

She left the wheelchair with Kay and headed round to the staffroom and tried not to get excited but, unlike on her coffee break when she'd last checked, there was now a present under the tree.

But it was in the shape of a Christmas stocking but, worse, it was the wrapped in the same paper as the ones in the storeroom.

Holly knew with a sinking feeling that, not wanting her to receive nothing, Kay had stepped in.

Deep down she had known full well that Daniel would forget.

Yet she had hoped he wouldn't.

And even now, as she opened the little attached card, she hoped for something that might indicate she was more than an afterthought.

That was all she was, Holly realised as she read the writing.

Holly Jacobs
Happy Christmas

Daniel could not have cared less if he'd tried to.

Don't cry here, Holly told herself, just make it out to the car. And so she came out of the staffroom and walked around to the department wearing a big smile and added her parcel to the pile on the wheel chair.

'What did you get?' Kay asked as Holly walked past her office.

'A chocolate stocking.'

'That's nice.' Kay smiled.

Had she not known that it was from Kay's secret stash then it might have been a perfectly nice gift.

But instead of nice it spoke volumes to Holly.

Holly said her goodbyes and headed off but as she came out of Emergency and to the main hospital entrance she was just in time to see Daniel walking back from wherever he had been.

'Have a great Christmas, Holly.'

'And you.'

And this was goodbye, Daniel knew.

He was staying just long enough to see Maddie for Christmas and sort out the tenants but then he would be gone.

And he was not coming back here again.

This was hurting him too.

'It's been great working with you,' Daniel said.

Seriously? Holly thought.

We had sex in my hall and that's the best you can do?

She pushed the wheelchair and kept on walking but then turned around and Daniel did too and they stared at each other. She could not believe he would just let her walk away so easily, that their final goodbye was a thank you for being a good colleague.

And so, when she should have left it at that, Holly revealed a little of what she held inside. 'A chocolate stocking?'

'Sorry?'

'You couldn't even be bothered to go to the gift shop. Instead, you had to get something from the store cupboard to give to me. I think I deserved a bit more than that!'

For a moment he stood there but then, remembering the rules she had told him about Secret Santa, Daniel frowned.

'How did you know it was from me?'

'Because...' Holly said, and then wished that she'd never started this.

Oh, she wished, how she wished that she'd never swapped around their names in the first place.

An incredulous smile spread over his face and he

pointed to her as realisation dawned. 'You rigged Secret Santa.'

'I did not! I was organising it so I had to know who got—'

'Liar,' Daniel broke in. 'You rigged it. Why would you do that?'

'Because...' Holly said for the second time, only this time she continued to speak. Actually, this time she made an already bad situation worse! 'I was hoping to find out how you felt.'

'Felt?'

'About us,' Holly said.

'Us?'

'Not *us*, in that sense,' she hurriedly amended. 'Just that it felt like more than a one-night stand.'

She should be shot on the spot for admitting it, Holly knew, she should take her heart right off her sleeve and pop it back in her chest.

Holly couldn't roll like that with him, though. Somehow with Daniel she was her honest worst.

'What do you mean by more?' Daniel asked.

Holly decided that silence really was her best defence now.

More meant more!

She had glimpsed *them*.

Oh, she would work on her New Year's resolutions and become all aloof and sophisticated next year, but there was still a few days until then.

'Holly,' he calmly stated. 'We had a great night. Can't you just enjoy it for what it was?'

There was a chill coming up the corridor as the automatic doors slid open and closed. The floor was wet as people trudged in with wet shoes and dripping umbrellas and romance was, for Holly, officially dead.

'Enjoy your gap year,' Holly said.

'Gap year?'

'Isn't that what it is?' Holly jeered. Well, she attempted a jeer, but she wasn't very good at being mean. 'Isn't that what teenagers do when they want to sort themselves out?'

Daniel, on the other hand, was very good at being mean and he thought of her love of winter weddings and the dreamy look that came over her at times. He was standing looking at a woman who would rig Secret Santa to find out how he *felt*. And, far from telling her that he was feeling far too much of late, instead Daniel's words tumbled out on a sneer. 'Say hi to him for me.'

'Who?'

'Mr Holly,' Daniel said, and basically accused her of being on husband watch. 'Clearly that's what you're looking for. It was supposed to be a bit of fun.'

Fun!

And with that word he did Holly a huge favour, for he snapped any lingering hope that remained, like an icy twig in the park.

'Well, have a *fun* Christmas,' Holly said, and did her best, with a rickety wheelchair piled high with gifts, to stalk off.

And he let her go.

Daniel watched her walk towards the car park and told himself that he was well shot of some stalker who would rig Secret Santa and a woman who looked for deeper meaning in everything...

Then as he walked back into the department and as the world carried on around him, he regretted how they had ended.

Yes, there was another gift for her that she would find

perhaps later tonight, but there would be no chance of them speaking by then.

He couldn't even drop by her flat after his shift to apologise as she was heading straight to her parents'.

Daniel was very aware that most of his thirty-two Christmases had been ruined somehow and now he'd just gone and ruined Holly's.

'Let it go,' he said under his breath, and picked up a patient file.

He couldn't let it go, though.

'Where are you going?' Kay asked as he put down the file and went to walk off.

'I'll be back in a few moments.'

Yes, he really should have let it go, Daniel thought as he strode through the car park. It was freezing outside and pouring with rain and he was just wearing scrubs and no doubt he'd already missed her.

But he hadn't.

There was Holly, sitting in the driver's seat of her car, and she was hunched over the steering wheel and in floods of tears.

'Holly…' He knocked on the window and she looked up and in horror saw who it was, and got back to clutching the steering wheel and started crying some more.

It felt to Holy like humiliation heaped on humiliation, especially when he chose to be nice and came around the other side and climbed into the passenger seat.

She heard his sigh, felt his awkwardness and smelt the delicious scent of him.

'I am not crying about you.' Holly told him the truth, or part of it—for she was not solely crying about him, more the utter disaster of her Christmas Eve. 'My car won't start…' She turned the key to show that this time she wasn't lying and it emitted a terrible sound.

'Don't flood the engine...' he warned, as it choked and gasped its last.

'There's a lot that needs fixing,' Holly said. 'I've been putting it off.'

She knew she couldn't complain about her car breaking down. It was terribly old and had been on its last legs for the last six months but it had always seen her safely home.

Till now.

'I have to get home, though...' She was seriously panicking—the trains were a disaster on Christmas Eve and she had no idea how she'd manage getting all the presents home. 'I can't miss it. I'll call a taxi...'

'Holly...' Daniel just didn't get it. Yes, he was aware that he had little family to speak of but Holly was at the other extreme. If she had five kids waiting for their mother he might understand more. 'These things happen. A taxi, if you can even get one to agree to take you, would cost a small fortune. As well as that you'd then have to get back for tomorrow night and there are no trains on Christmas Day.'

'I can borrow my mum's car to get back.'

'Can't you just miss it?'

'We're not all like you,' Holly said. It was far easier to carry on being mean. 'Some of us want to be with our family at Christmas.' And then she stopped gripping the steering wheel and leant back as the need to score points faded and the truth came in. 'My mum's not very well...'

She'd told him that, Daniel remembered. She just hadn't revealed how sick her mother was.

Now she did.

'Why didn't you tell Kay?'

'She knows,' Holly said. 'Last year I had both Christmas and New Year off. Mum's actually doing better lately. This was supposed to be the real happy Christmas after the fake happy Christmas last year. To tell the truth, it's all a bit strained at home, Mum's become rather too used to getting her own way.' Holly took a breath. 'She's going to have to understand that these things happen...'

'Will she, though?'

'Probably not.' Holly actually smiled and then wiped all the tears away with the sleeve of her coat and looked over to where he sat and saw that he was wearing only thin scrubs and that his hair was all wet from the rain.

'Why did you come out?' Holly asked him. 'Did I forget to sign something?'

'No. I came out because I hated that we ended things on a row.'

'So do I.'

'I think we can both do better than that,' Daniel said. 'Why don't I drive you home? I don't finish till four but—'

'I can't ask you to do that.'

'You didn't ask,' he pointed out.

'It's Christmas Eve...' Holly flailed, yet he was calm.

'Hence the emergency.'

And it was an emergency, at least it was to Holly.

'How far away do you live?' Daniel asked.

'Three hours on a good day. Four if it's...' she looked out of the window and saw the sheets of rain and factored in the Christmas traffic. 'It might even be five.'

'That's okay, but I won't stay,' he warned.

'I know.'

'Just let's get you home.'

'Thank you.'

'Do we have to carry all the presents back into the department?' Daniel asked, and Holly laughed.

'No.'

It was decided that they would lock them up in his rather more secure car and Holly would take the underground home.

'I'll come and pick you up as soon as I finish.'

'Thanks.'

'Go and eat some chocolate,' Daniel said.

'Oh, I shall.' She held up the blasted chocolate stocking and they both shared a smile. 'I've got plenty after all.'

Holly, as she headed for home, was thrilled with the thought of a few more hours with him because Daniel was right...

They deserved better than to end it on a row.

CHAPTER NINE

DANIEL WORKED THROUGH the afternoon and at two he took a call from the acute medical unit.

'What time did Albert Marlesford's family say that they'd be here?'

'His niece had some shopping to do,' Daniel explained. 'I told him that she must be busy and to stop fretting.'

Daniel ended the call and told his cynical self to be quiet.

Of course Dianne would be in, he had spoken to her himself.

He was worried for the old boy, though.

'Shouldn't you be off?' Kay checked a while later, and Daniel glanced at the time.

'I should be and I am,' Daniel said. 'And this time it's for good. It's been an absolutely pleasure to work with you Kay.'

It really had been.

So much so that once he'd got his head sorted out, Daniel was wondering if, maybe a year or so from now, he'd be back—and not as a locum. But there was too much going on in his mind right now to voice very tentative thoughts.

And neither would it be fair to Holly to say he was considering returning someday.

'Don't forget your present,' Kay reminded him.

He went to the tree and there was a little parcel wrapped in silver with a curly bow. If Holly had rigged the Secret Santa so that he would get her name then presumably she had chosen a present for him.

He checked the attached card and saw her loopy handwriting.

'Open it,' Kay said.

'Later.'

He didn't go straight to the car; instead, he took his cynical self up to the acute medical unit and found that Albert's relatives still hadn't arrived.

Albert was comfortable, they said.

Sleeping.

And that was surely better than the streets but for a moment there Daniel had entered a world where families reunited.

After that he walked out to the car. It was already starting to get dark and he really should press on. Yet he sat for a moment in the driver's seat and wondered what she had bought and what had been written on the card but, rather than find out now, Daniel put it in his glove box. This journey had the potential to be awkward enough, without finding out that she'd bought him a little Holly & Daniel snow globe or...

Well, he didn't possess much imagination in the romantic Christmas present department. Still, he would guess that if she was *that* upset about the stocking, well, there was going to be something rather special for him in that silver parcel.

He'd open it tomorrow, Daniel decided. He'd open it when she was safely home.

Safely, because he liked her.

More than he cared to admit to himself and certainly more than he dared to admit to Holly.

Of course she was confused, because so too was he. For the best part of a year Daniel had been planning for this trip and desperate to get away.

Now, though, it felt as if there were more and more reasons to stay.

Daniel pulled up outside her flat and did his best not to recall chasing her up the concrete stairs, and as he knocked on the door he tried not to remember them falling through it.

'Come in.' Holly beamed.

'I'd better not,' Daniel said. He really, given what had taken place there, didn't want to stand in the hall! 'The traffic sounds pretty bad.'

'Of course…' She was a little flustered. 'I'll be one moment.'

He stood on the doorstep and then realised that Holly was on the telephone and so, rather than being like his father who would sit in the car, pressing on the horn until everyone came out, he stepped in and waved a hand as if to say to take her time.

Holly headed into her bedroom, which was really her living room. She had the television on, he could see, though the sound was turned down.

'We're just leaving now,' he heard Holly saying. 'No, don't worry about that. I'll see you shortly.' Then another pause. 'Mum, I really do have to go. Daniel's already doing me a huge favour.' She came to the bedroom door and rolled her eyes. Clearly her mother thought there was a lot that had to be discussed between now and three hours' time when Holly would be there.

'Yes, I've got the cheese,' Holly said.

So, rather than drumming his fingers and appearing impatient, Daniel went through to a small lounge room and took a seat and listened to the neighbours shouting.

'Sorry about that,' Holly said as she came through to the rather cold lounge. 'The logistics of Christmas in my family. Honestly…' She blew out a breath and picked up a coat from the chair. 'I'm ready.'

'I'm not,' Daniel admitted. 'I'd love a drink.'

'Sure.' Holly said. 'Coffee?'

'Please.'

He followed her into the kitchen.

'Do you want something to eat?'

And usually he would say no, but he hadn't had lunch and, given that he had no intention of stopping on the drive to her home, it would be a long time until he'd be eating again.

'Thanks.'

She made toasted sandwiches. Turkey, Brie and cranberry.

'It's Christmas after all.'

They smelt delicious.

'Now I can see the end of my movie.'

It wasn't a plan to get him into the bedroom, Daniel knew, given that she practically lived there.

And so she flicked the television back on and it was one of those stupid movies that ran every Christmas.

'Holly,' Daniel said, 'even I know the ending.'

She just smiled and sat on the edge of the bed to eat her own toasted sandwiches while Daniel took a seat on a small chair, though, rather disconcerting for him was this sudden wish to lie down and open a bottle of wine and watch the movie and…

…spend Christmas in bed.

'I love this bit.' She turned up the sound on the movie

as they ate and even Daniel laughed, because it was cheesy and funny and it was just very, very nice to be here.

'Did Albert's family come and visit him?'

'Albert?' Daniel checked, and then shook his head. 'How would I know?'

'I thought they might have popped into Emergency, or that you might have…' She gave him a smile. 'I bet they're having a good old catch-up right now.'

Daniel didn't return her smile; instead, he stood.

'Come on, we'd better go.'

The traffic was hell and the car inched its way through the streets but finally they hit the motorway.

Then the car stopped inching its way.

It just sat in gridlocked traffic as both pretended not to notice it was now after six.

'What are your plans for tomorrow?' asked Holly, just trying to be polite.

'No definite plans,' Daniel said.

'Will you see your family?'

'I'll pop in for ten minutes.'

He briefly turned and saw her rapid blink and saw the wrestle as she tried not to judge.

'Things are a bit complicated at home,' he said, when usually he offered no reason.

Thankfully the traffic eased a little and for the next hour they made if not good then reasonable time.

The phone rang out in the car, making her jump as it came over the speakers, and she glanced at the dash.

Dad.

Daniel didn't answer the call.

Then five minutes later it happened again and she could feel the tension in him.

There were signs for a service station and guessing

he might want to speak to his father without having it broadcast over the speakers for her to hear Holly asked if they could stop.

'Holly...' He glanced at the time on the dashboard. 'We need to push on.'

'And I need the loo.'

He gritted his teeth as they pulled into the service station and Holly got out. 'Do you want anything?' she offered.

'To get there this year. Just hurry.'

He watched her disappear into the building and then realising he could call his father Daniel did so. He kept an eye out for Holly as he was connected and they briefly spoke.

'Amelia's trying to sort out numbers for dinner...'

Daniel let out a silent mirthless laugh. From the way his father described it Amelia was counting out potatoes and fretting as to whether she had enough, when, in truth, she'd just give the number expected for dinner to the maid.

And as he sat there he could well recall coming home from boarding school where Christmas preparations had been in full swing to a house where there were none.

His father had often worked and no matter how nice the nanny was, she would far rather be on the phone to her own family on Christmas Day than entertaining him.

And he remembered with clarity the loneliness of Christmas and he was so over the pretence and the farce of it all.

'I shan't be there for dinner,' he told his father. 'I'll drop by with Maddie's present but I really can't stay for long.'

'We'll be going to the club in the afternoon...'

Daniel opened his mouth to say something, but wasn't

sure it was his place. At least his father made some effort now, at least, for Christmas he tried to be home.

'When do you fly?'

'I still haven't booked,' Daniel admitted.

He didn't know if he wanted to go.

Holly was right.

Thirty-two was pretty old to be taking a gap year.

He was running and a little like Albert he was suddenly tired. 'I'll see you tomorrow,' Daniel said.

'Maddie wants to speak to you.'

'Tell Maddie I'll see her tomorrow,' Daniel told his father, because he could see Holly making her way back to the car. 'I have to go.'

Despite his telling Holly to hurry, she had taken the time to stop for refreshments and he had to reach out and open the door as she was carrying two take-away cups.

'Christmas coffee!' Holly smiled, handing him one of the cups and then climbing in.

'You find the Christmas in everything.'

'I do.

He took a sip and pulled a face. 'What the hell is this?'

'Coffee and cinnamon, I think,' Holly said. 'And maybe a bit of nutmeg?' Then she got to the real reason she had taken so long. 'Did you call him?

And one of the reasons she irked him and one of the reasons he liked her more than she knew was because of moments like this—Holly had done the polite thing, Daniel now realised. Guessing that he might not want her around while he spoke with his father, she had made a polite excuse to leave.

Then she had ruined her tact by asking if he had called him!

'Yes,' Daniel said. 'He just wanted to check on numbers for dinner.'

'Are you going?'

'No,' Daniel said as they again hit the motorway.

'I'm sure he'd love it if you came along...'

Daniel said nothing and Holly could sense he'd prefer it if she didn't either.

'I'll leave it,' she offered.

'Please do.'

He stared at the car registration in front of him and then at the wall of traffic ahead and, of course, Holly simply could not leave it.

'But surely at Christmas...'

'Holly.' Daniel turned. 'I didn't offer you a lift home to indulge in a cosy chat about my family situation. I don't need your take on it.'

'Friends talk...' Holly started, and then gave in. Who had even said they were friends?

She didn't even have his phone number and he had never asked for hers.

'I wonder when it will stop raining,' Holly said, and Daniel rolled his eyes at her attempt at conversation. 'Is that banal enough for you? We can talk like strangers at a bus stop.'

'Holly...'

'I mean, it's not as if we're even friends. You couldn't even be bothered to introduce me to your ex.'

He knew she was referring to Amelia.

'She's not my ex.'

Holly rolled her eyes. 'An old one-night stand, then.'

'I've never slept with her.'

'I don't believe you.'

'You don't have to believe me, Holly.' God, she had a nerve. 'I don't have to explain myself to you.'

He wanted to, though.

It had been excruciating in the department store and

it had been that way for Holly too and no doubt why she had decided to walk off.

'I know it was awkward for you at the shop...'

'It was awkward long before that,' Holly sighed. 'Maddie called three times when you were in the shower. Was she your date the other day?' When he didn't answer she stared out of the passenger window. 'Honestly, Daniel, I don't know how you juggle them all.'

Then again, he hadn't attempted to juggle or hide, Holly thought, he'd just listened to his messages while she'd sat there, pulling on her boots.

'Amelia, the woman you met that day is my stepmum.'

To her credit, Holly said nothing, not even a little shocked gasp. She just turned back to look at him.

'That date I had last week was with my sister, Maddie.'

'Maddie's your sister?'

'Yes, and she's five.'

'Why didn't you just say?'

'Because I find it awkward. When we're out everyone assumes that she's mine.'

'Is that why you're still here?' Holly asked, and looked at him.

'Yes, she wanted me to see her in the nativity play and she's getting upset about me going away.'

'You'd be like a rock star to her.'

Daniel nodded. 'It's not all one-way, she's actually very good company. We go to the movies and things but I don't really go over to the house.'

'Because you don't get on with your dad?' Holly frowned. 'Surely you can get past that for her sake?'

And then his phone rang again and she glanced at the dash.

Maddie.

'What's she doing up this late?' Daniel asked, though more to himself.

'It's Christmas Eve.' Holly answered anyway! 'She's probably excited.'

When he answered the call, though, Maddie sounded a little strained.

'Is Father Christmas real?' she asked him. 'Thomas said it's all made up.'

'Thomas?' Daniel checked.

'He was Joseph in the nativity play.'

'The one with no teeth?' Daniel checked, and Maddie started to laugh. 'The one who nearly dropped the baby? I wouldn't be paying too much attention to him.'

'So there is a Father Christmas?'

'Yes.' He could say that because for all Amelia's faults she would make sure there were presents under the tree for her daughter. 'So you can stop worrying and go to bed and I'll see you tomorrow.'

'For dinner?'

'Not for dinner, I'm...' He could feel Holly's ears on elastic as she pretended not to listen and he couldn't even come up with an excuse. 'I'll see you tomorrow.'

'Why can't you just go for dinner?' Holly said once the call had ended. 'I mean, how hard could it be?'

'Holly, my father didn't even celebrate Christmas until he married Amelia. I used to sit at home with the nanny on her phone the entire day to her family overseas while he went to work.'

She knew she was hearing the truth, there was something in his voice that told her that Christmas had always been hell.

'Not all families are perfect, Holly!'

She could hear the dig and she stared ahead.

'My family's not perfect, Daniel.'

'Well, they come close.' Daniel mimicked her voice when she'd spoken about her birthday. '"My parents always make sure that both are celebrated!"' He reverted to his bitterness. 'Of course they do.'

'Not always.' And she stared ahead at the traffic and she told him a truth, and this time it was Holly who was more speaking to herself. 'They forgot my birthday once.'

CHAPTER TEN

'When you say "Forgot…"?'

'They forgot completely,' Holly said.

'Tell me.'

'No.' Holly shook her head. 'You've just admitted that you basically had no Christmas at all growing up, so it seems a bit shallow to be upset about missing out on one birthday.'

'How old were you?' Daniel asked.

'I was six, turning seven.'

So not a whole lot older than Maddie was now, and he could just imagine the hurt it would cause his little sister.

'Tell me,' he said, and his voice was kind and she found that she wanted to.

Silly, that some silly childhood memory could make her eyes burn all these years later.

'Usually we had birthday cake for breakfast on Christmas Day and I opened my presents and then we'd all go through to the lounge and Christmas Day would start. We still do that, though we have champagne now too. It was just one year…' Her voice trailed off as she recalled her confusion when they'd gone straight through to the lounge. And how she'd tried not to cry as she'd opened her presents. 'I kept thinking they were just pretending that they'd forgotten and then I realised they actually had.

Now I look back I can see it had been a difficult year for my mum. My Uncle Harry had been in hospital—he'll be there tomorrow… Drunkle Harry.'

Daniel smiled.

'And Adam, my brother, had been sick with bronchiolitis.'

'When did they remember?'

'When I went to bed. Mum came in to say goodnight.'

'Were you crying?'

'No, I had my nervous smile on!' Holly said, and they both laughed but then both fell silent.

She stared out of the window, recalling that odd day, and she knew that the tears in her eyes had little to do with some long-ago memory.

It was a little like how Daniel made her feel now.

As if something that was so terribly important to her meant very little to him.

If she hadn't pushed that envelope under his nose, if Kay hadn't prompted him, she'd be minus a chocolate stocking now.

Exactly!

And while, yes, he'd come out to make up for their row, if her car hadn't broken down they'd have already gone their separate ways by now.

Soon she would be forgotten.

Finally his chirpy passenger was silent and Daniel got the peace he had craved, except he rather missed her incessant chatter.

The traffic was barely moving and to fill the silence he turned the radio on and listened to the carols.

Another half a mile, another half an hour.

And still Holly said nothing.

She took out some Christmas cards from her bag and

started to write them but after a couple she gave in and put them in the door pocket. She was tired of being peppy and ensuring that everyone was happy.

Blue lights were flashing up the hard shoulder, though it was the police and fire brigade that were passing them, rather than ambulances.

'Have a look on your phone,' Daniel said, 'and see what's happening.'

'A lorry has lost its load,' Holly said.

'We might need to think about getting off at the next exit.'

'We can't,' Holly said as she went through the traffic updates. 'There's flash flooding and the exit is closed.'

And she expected a hiss of frustration from Daniel but instead he gave a soft laugh. 'Of course it is.' He looked ahead. 'We might have to find somewhere to stay the night.'

'I'm really sorry for messing up your Christmas,' Holly said.

'There was no Christmas to mess up.'

'Oh, that's right, it's just another day.'

She simply could not get how she could be so crazy about someone who cared so little about the things that mattered to her and she actually told him so.

'I'm glad that we're not going anywhere,' Holly said.

'It might start moving.'

'I'm not talking about the traffic,' Holly admitted, and raised the awkward subject in the hope of clearing the air. 'I'm talking about my mythical us.'

Daniel smiled.

'You'd buy me shoes or something for Christmas.'

'I would,' Daniel said, and then frowned. 'Don't women like shoes?'

'Not the flat work ones that you'd get for me. No, it

would be a combined Christmas and birthday present that I'd get from you and one of those horrible cheap cards.'

'I don't do cards.'

'Exactly!' Holly said, and then she sighed. 'I'm sorry I didn't stick to my end of the deal. I always knew I'd be lousy at one-night stands. I really need to loosen up.'

'Then do.'

'It's easier said than done.'

'It is easy, though,' Daniel told her. 'Just think of sex as fun.'

He'd used the F-word again but now it made her smile.

'How?'

'You just don't go looking for a deeper meaning in everything, just, as they say, enjoy the ride.'

'Ha-ha.'

'So what did you get me for Christmas?' Daniel asked, because he really was curious to know.

'Didn't you even open it?'

'Nope.'

'Then you can find out tomorrow. What did you get for Maddie?'

'The necklace you didn't like,' Daniel said.

'I didn't know then that she was five! She'll love it.'

'I hope so. And she'll find out tomorrow that she's adopted an elephant.'

'What did you get for your father?'

'A book.'

'Amelia?'

'A diary.'

Holly screwed up her nose.

'We don't get on.'

'Have you ever tried?'

'Once,' Daniel said. 'Not at first, though. My father and I fell out when he started dating Amelia. I didn't approve of the age difference. I found it embarrassing actually, and it was clear to me she was just there for the money. Still, once Maddie was born I decided to make more effort...'

'Because you realised they were in love?'

'No, Polly,' Daniel said, and turned and smiled. 'Because Amelia is as shallow as my father is distant and I wanted someone to actually be present for the child.'

The traffic was at a complete standstill. She could see the red brake lights snaking for miles into the distance and the car moved forward about a hand space every five minutes or so.

'I worry about Maddie,' he admitted. 'She's being raised by nannies and neither of them could be bothered to show up for her nativity play.' Daniel gripped the wheel. 'He just doesn't get it.'

'Have you spoken to him?'

Daniel said nothing.

Well, he had been about to give a derisive laugh and say something like 'As if that's going to change anything,' but instead he stayed silent as he thought some more about doing just that.

Again.

'I tried to when she was born,' Daniel admitted. 'It probably wasn't the best time. I had just turned down a surgical position in favour of Emergency. He told me that just as I clearly didn't want career advice from him, likewise he didn't need parenting advice.'

'It sounds like he does.'

The Christmas carols were still playing on the radio, all happy and jolly, and it was Holly who turned it off.

'Thanks.'

Daniel actually appreciated it.

'Why are you leaving?' Holly asked. 'It sounds like you want to be there for your sister.'

'I do,' he agreed. 'But I can't be.'

He knew she didn't understand so he decided to explain. After all, there was no chance of her ever meeting Amelia. 'I really tried to put aside my doubts about the marriage. Last year my father was working and I took Maddie and Amelia to a pantomime and I did all the big-brother stuff. Then Amelia said she wanted to decorate Maddie's room as a surprise and could I help pick out some paper...'

'What did you say?' Holly asked, and her antennae were up.

He could almost see them rising out of her fluffy dark hair and homing in, and, Daniel thought, for someone so sweet she was also rather shrewd.

'I said, no, that there were interior designers for all that and I chalked it up as odd but...' He held out his hand and made a wavy sign that said that the jury had remained out about the small incident but it had seemed odd at the time.

Holly nodded to show she agreed with his take on things.

'Then last Christmas I was invited over, as I have been for the past couple of years. I generally go for dinner, and for Maddie's birthdays and things. Her family were there and Amelia was a bit tense and hitting the mulled wine and then brandy, and then...'

'What happened?'

'I fell asleep on the sofa and while I was gone her family went home, Maddie went for a sleep and my father went to his club. I woke up and she was sitting beside where I lay and she said she was miserable and that though the money was lovely and everything he was old and she wanted young and, well, he'd never have to find out...'

Oh! She wanted to open the car door and get out onto the freezing motorway just to cool her cheeks.

'We didn't do anything.'

'I never asked.'

'Well, just so you know. Anyway, I don't really need you to believe me.' Actually, he did. 'Even if I'd wanted to, which I didn't, there would have been serious technical issues.'

'So, what did you say to her?'

'Not much.' Daniel sat silent for a moment as he recalled it. 'I told her it wouldn't be happening and got my jacket and went home. Since then I do my best to stay away.'

'I see.'

'Until September this year I worked at the same hospital as my father so it was pretty easy to find out what was going on and to only go over if Amelia was away. She goes on a lot of trips,' Daniel explained. 'I actually hadn't seen her since that day until the department store.'

'Okay, you're forgiven for not introducing me.'

He turned and she was wearing a smile, though not a nervous one.

'Embarrassing, isn't it?' he said.

'For her, I guess,' Holly said. 'Did you tell your father?'

'Good God, no!' Daniel sounded shocked at the very thought. 'I think I have to just accept that I'm not very good at family Christmases.'

'Oh, I don't know about that,' Holly said. 'You didn't do anything wrong, your father doesn't know and your little sister's none the wiser. I'd say you handled it all rather well.'

Daniel gave a small laugh.

No one knew, and certainly he hadn't envisaged telling anyone, but now that he had he felt lighter.

Holly, though, was grumbling as she again checked her phone for a traffic report.

'I'm starting to think I wasn't meant to get home for Christmas.'

'So is everyone else who is stuck in the jam,' Daniel said, and then he was practical, 'We can get off the motorway at the next available exit and try and find somewhere to stay the night or we can press on.'

It was long after ten p.m. A three-hour trip had already turned into six.

'I don't want to ruin your Christmas,' Holly started, and then thought about the long drive home he would have tomorrow. 'I've already ruined it.'

'Holly.' Daniel looked over and but Holly didn't look back, she was till reading the road report on her phone as if staring at it might make things change.

Her Christmas earrings had almost stopped flashing. Like the black box missing in a plane they still emitted the occasional hopeful bleep that Christmas cheer could still be found.

And they were right to hope, for Daniel found himself telling her something truly real…

'This is the nicest Christmas I've ever had.'

CHAPTER ELEVEN

'I NEED TO go to the loo.'

He had guessed she might because she'd kept crossing and uncrossing her legs.

'You went at the service station.'

'And then I drank both of the coffees.'

People were actually pulling over to sort out the essentials but there was no way Holly would be joining them.

Tonight, when she looked back on it, would be embarrassing enough as it was, without her pale moon rising.

'I think it's time we gave in,' Daniel conceded.

Another exit was coming up and it was now or never.

As they inched towards the exit Holly started ringing around local motels and bed and breakfasts from the list that came up on her phone.

'No room at the inn.' She sighed, because it would seem half of their fellow commuters had beaten them to it.

'No *rooms*,' Daniel pointed out, because Holly was trying to find two. 'The first one said that they had a double room.' He saw her jaw tense at the prospect of the two of them and one double bed. 'I've been driving for six hours, having worked all day,' Daniel said. 'I'm tired and I'm hungry. I can assure you that you could get up and pole dance and I wouldn't notice. Still, if you want, you can have the sofa.'

'What if there isn't one?'

'Then you can have the floor.'

'You're such a gentleman.'

'No, Holly, I'm not.'

With little choice Holly rang back and secured the room and a short while later the car pulled into a bed and breakfast. By now she was past caring if the presents got pinched and so thankfully didn't suggest they haul everything inside.

And he was very pleased that the snowman bag remained safely locked in the car.

Daniel did the checking in and Holly dashed to the loo and then returned to his side, pleased to find that the formalities were over. Daniel was talking to a woman whom he introduced as Mrs Barrett.

No, the formalities were not over!

She proceeded to repeat to Holly all the rules she had just told Daniel.

'No noise after midnight.'

'We really just want to crash…' Holly agreed.

'No parties in the room.'

'Honestly,' Holly said.

'Just let her finish,' Daniel broke in, and it became clear he had tried to hurry Mrs Barrett along a few moments before but to no avail.

There were to be no showers after midnight, clothes were to be worn between the bathroom and bedroom, and shoes were to be taken off and carried up the stairs and not left in the hall and…

'You need to sign the register every time you enter and leave,' Mrs Barrett informed Holly as she handed her a pen.

They took off their shoes and were led up some very creaky stairs.

'Breakfast is between seven and nine, no latecomers.'

'We'll be gone by seven,' Daniel said. 'Is there anywhere we can call to get pizza or…?'

'No.' Mrs Barrett shook her head and no helpful suggestions ensued.

'I'm starving,' Daniel mouthed to Holly, and she laughed.

'Here…' Mrs Barrett inserted a key and pushed open a door, and it was like entering a time slip because nothing in this room could have changed in thirty or so years. It was all crinoline and purple and there were little doilies on every available surface.

And there was no sofa!

'How much do I owe you?' Holly asked once they were alone.

'It's my treat,' Daniel said, and smiled a black smile because, really, this was far from the Ritz. 'Holly, I *have* to eat something.'

'I've got some cheeses in the car in a cool bag,' Holly said. 'And some chocolate…'

'We can have a picnic.'

'Oh, and I got my father some Scotch for Christmas, I'm sure he won't mind. I'll go,' Holly said, 'I know where everything is.'

'No, I'll go,' Daniel said, and picked up his keys. There was no way he wanted her going through the bags.

Daniel went back down and spoke with Mrs Barrett and he even managed a wry smile as she asked him to sign out.

He went to the car and found the cool bag and a present that was clearly a bottle of Scotch and then went back up to the room, threw himself on the bed and stretched out.

'Finally.'

Clearly he would not be giving up the bed!

'I had to sign in and out just to go to the car.'

There were two glasses on a little table with a jug of water and Holly poured them both a measure of Scotch and started to plate up the cheese.

Daniel headed off and had a shower and came back wearing only his underwear.

'You're supposed to be dressed when you come out of the bathroom,' Holly reminded him.

'Well, I would have had I had a change of clothes.'

Soon she was sitting on the floor as Daniel hung off the bed and they ate and drank and chatted and laughed.

It was nice.

More than that, it was the nicest Christmas Eve she had ever spent because, cheese and Scotch aside, Daniel was one of her favourite things, especially when he was half-naked.

He asked a bit about her family.

'Do you get on with your brother?' Daniel asked, and Holly nodded. 'Stupid question—you get on with everyone.'

'Not everyone.' And because he'd asked about her family, now she asked about his. 'Do you remember your mum?'

'A bit.' He nodded. 'She was the one who always made the effort at Christmas and things...'

'What was it like after she died?'

'I went to boarding school,' Daniel said. 'And, to be honest, I preferred being there than at home. It was miserable.'

'Maybe he was grieving?'

'Maybe,' Daniel said. He'd never really thought of it like that. 'I went to Rupert's one Christmas.'

'The one you were best man for?' Holly asked, and Daniel nodded.

'He's a good friend. When I was all set to boycott my father's wedding he talked me round. I guess that I went helps keep things, at least outwardly, civilised.'

'What was Christmas like at Rupert's?'

He shrugged. 'They were all really into Christmas, a bit like your family, I guess.'

'Did you enjoy it?'

'Not really,' Daniel admitted. 'I guess it just showed more clearly all that was missing in mine. I think things are very different for Maddie, though. Not perfect, of course, but a lot better.'

And he knew too that things were better still for Maddie when he was around.

'If you want a shower then you'd better go now,' Daniel glanced at the time. 'It's close to midnight.'

Holly headed out to the shower and had a very quick one and then realised she'd forgotten her pyjamas. She got exactly what Daniel meant about putting on old clothes so she wrapped herself in a towel and legged it back to the bedroom, but as she stepped in she saw that it was in darkness except for a candle.

'Happy birthday, Holly.'

'You remembered!'

'I did.'

'I'd actually forgotten that it was my birthday.'

'No, you hadn't.'

'I honestly had,' Holly said. 'Aren't you going to sing?'

'Nope.'

She knelt down and blew out her candle and found out that it was held in a little piece of carrot cake with orange and cream cheese frosting.

'I got it from Mrs Barrett when I went down for the

cheese,' Daniel explained. 'She warned me again that
there were to be no parties after midnight.'

'We'll be quiet, then.'

'You can eat the frosting.'

Holly did and Daniel knelt down too and he had the
cake, but one wasn't the same without the other and for
that reason *only* they shared a little kiss.

They both tasted perfect.

It was just a simple kiss but both fought the urge to
rip off each other's towel.

'Thank you,' Holly said, trying to pretend she wasn't
turned on, 'for making it such a lovely birthday.'

'I haven't finished yet.' He got up and turned on the
bedside light. 'You've got to open your present.'

'Present?'

'Yes.'

Her present was on the bed and wrapped in lilac tissues from a box that, incidentally, had a purple knitted
cover over it.

The bedroom really was a treasure trove of nylon and
knits.

'Oh, my!' Holly said when she opened it. Her present
was a lovely leather wallet. A little used perhaps, but,
actually, it was something of his, and while Holly was a
little confused, she still said the right thing for appear-
ances' sake.

'I can't take your wallet.'

'It's more what's inside that is yours,' he told her.
'Open it up.'

There was some cash.

'Count it.'

There wasn't very much, a couple of notes and some
coins, and he made a little pile on the bedside table.

'Can you get your hair done for that?' Daniel asked.

'Er, no.'

'Your nails?'

'No.' Holly laughed at the very notion. He really didn't have a clue.

'I'm trying to be thoughtful,' Daniel chided her mirth. 'Could you maybe get a nail polish?'

'Indeed I could.' Holly beamed. 'I could get two, in fact.'

'Well, then, you can do your nails on me.'

'Thank you.'

'Keep looking.'

'There's nothing else...' Holly said, and then her voice trailed off when her fingers found something shiny and silver and she went to hand his wallet back to him. 'You didn't empty it out properly.'

'I did.'

'No.' Holly shook her head. 'You didn't.' She took out a condom. 'You're such a slut, Daniel. You forgot to take this out.'

'No, Holly, I didn't.'

Her cheeks were on fire as he continued to speak.

'One night, just for you...'

'That's such a generous present,' Holly said. 'So self-less.'

'I know. I can be nice like that at times.'

'I mean, you'd have sex with me just because it's my birthday...'

'Not just sex,' Daniel said. 'This would be just-for-Holly sex.'

'So you won't enjoy it?'

'That's not you for you to concern yourself with. Your wish, or rather your birthday wish, would be my command.'

'Just some fun?' Holly checked.

'Exactly!'

'I don't think so.' She shook her head. 'I thought you said that even if I was naked and dancing…'

'I meant it when I said it.' Daniel broke in. 'But that got me thinking about just that…'

'No.'

'Well, the offer is there, just tear the edge off that little wrapper and I'll appear!'

He got into bed.

And she put on tartan pyjama bottoms and a little top that were fine for home but not exactly Daniel Chandler worthy and climbed into bed beside him.

She lay on her back more than a little miffed by his gift offer but also intrigued at the concept of her wish being his command. 'You could be skiing down a mountain one minute and then diving head-first between my legs the next…'

'I'm not a genie, Holly.' He pulled her into his lovely, warm body. 'The gift offer expires at seven a.m. *Then* it's Christmas.'

'Why would you rot things up now?' she asked. 'It's taken three weeks to be talking and it would take us straight back to awkward again.'

'But it wouldn't,' Daniel said. 'I'd just be showing you how to loosen up. You say tomato…'

Holly frowned. 'I don't get it.'

'You call it making love, whereas I…'

'I don't call it making love.'

'You think of it as such.'

'Not really,' Holly said. 'Maybe a bit.'

He was right.

Oh, she wished Daniel wasn't. That she could just take out her heart and leave it on charge overnight, just as she had done with her phone. Yes, she wished she could say,

Go for it Daniel, have wicked sex with me all night and I shan't hurt when you leave me in the morning.

But she didn't work like that.

'The offer's there.'

'Noted.'

Because he clearly had no conscience, Daniel was soon asleep, whereas Holly lay there, listening to the sound of rain against the window and his heavy breathing.

His leg came over hers, but he wasn't making a move, it was just that he was tall and the bed was small.

And once she felt him harden and Holly lay there all nervous and tense and awaiting his pounce.

He didn't.

It was already the best birthday she had ever had!

CHAPTER TWELVE

Christmas morning

IT WAS COLD.

Not just cold, it was freezing.

So freezing that in sleep in they had rolled into the dint in the bed and wrapped themselves around each other, and for Daniel, who didn't really do the wrapped around you type of thing, or rather didn't usually, he woke for the second time with her in his arms and facing away from him.

She had on a little strappy top and pyjama bottoms yet his hand had found its way to her stomach and he went to remove it. His intent was to roll on his back so she didn't feel him hard against her, but then his hand chose to linger and then she stirred and it was a little too late for that.

Actually, it wasn't.

He could still roll onto his back now and then roll out of bed.

They could be up and packed and out of here and heading for her home.

Or he could kiss her shoulder as he had wanted to that morning all those weeks ago.

His hand was lightly stroking her stomach and he could feel that she was trying to keep her breathing even.

So too was he.

'Happy birthday, Holly.'

'Thank you.'

He was breathing through his nostrils in that delicious turned-on, decision-making way. Resisting and yet wanting.

She looked at the clock and saw it was just before seven.

And then everything went black because she closed her eyes to the feel of his mouth and the deep kiss that met her shoulder.

It was a slow, sensual kiss and his tongue was warm on her cold, bare skin and his hand slipped up her top and found her breast.

He toyed with her nipple and then rubbed her breast with his palm and his mouth moved up her neck to her ear so she could both hear and feel his ragged breathing.

Holly pressed her bottom back into him, just because she wanted more of the feel of him hard and turned on.

And Daniel too needed more because he slid the top up over her head, discarded it and then went back to her neck. He loved the feel of her now naked back against his chest.

Now his hand slid down further down and he listened to the throaty moans she made as he stroked her clitoris and delivered little volts of pleasure that had her thighs grip his hand.

And it was all about her yet he stopped just long enough that they both kicked off their bottoms halves. His free hand moved under her torso so he could play with her other breast.

He moved his hand down, sliding his fingers inside her. She could feel him nudging between her thighs, wet, warm and hard.

'Oh, God,' he said, but just quietly and not to her, and for a moment she wondered why. Then she understood, for he knew, even before Holly did, that she was about to come.

It was so intense that she brought her knees up.

There, the sensible part of him warned as she came to his hand. *Leave it there. Feel that bliss on your fingers and then smile and say Happy Birthday.*

It wasn't enough, though.

For either of them.

Her lovely birthday 'gift' hadn't left her sated, it had just made her hungry for more. She turned in his arms and they found each other's mouths briefly before he moved down to kiss her breasts, one by delicious one, tasting them for the first time.

Oh, that mouth, Holly thought as her fingers tangled in his hair. She wished he had two of them so he could keep kissing her breasts while also taking her mouth. His head followed the upward guide of her hand and their mouths met again in a kiss unplanned. Deep, slow and sensual, their tongues mingled and then their mouths parted in private focus as he entered her.

She moaned at the bliss of the slow long strokes that had her wrap one leg around him as they moved together.

They were kissing intensely, stopping only to stare into each other's eyes before kissing again. It was so real, so raw.

Daniel got up on his forearms just to watch her and she pressed her palms into his chest.

The tight, slick grip of her had Daniel revelling in the sensations and then the demand of his pace increased.

The shift in him started to tip her. Even when he had

taken her standing, fast and rough, he had been in measured control.

But now neither had hold of themselves, they were lost in each other. His hand came over her mouth and the sound of her affirmations were silenced. He felt the stretch of her smile on his palm as she realised the noises she'd been making. Daniel would usually have revelled in that but there was something about the simple sound of them, slick and in tune, intensely moving together that enraptured him. He forgot to smile, or to do anything other than focus hard…on her.

His breathing was ragged and hard in her ear as he pulled her deeper into oblivion.

Holly dug her fingers into taut buttocks and the fire low in his spine shot forward.

Her reward for silence? The deep moan of his release.

Heat met perfect heat and though she gripped and tightened and drew him in, as he shot into her, she also unfurled, for she opened herself up to him.

Those last thrusts were exquisite, those deep kisses, while still dizzy, were the most intense expression she had ever known. They coiled with each other, caressed each other, and their lips did not know how to part.

Until they did…

CHAPTER THIRTEEN

THEY LAY AFTERWARDS, both a little stunned by what had taken place.

She had never known just how beautiful sex could be and Daniel had done all he could not to find out.

The only sound now was the rain and they lay on their backs, idly holding hands as their breathing slowed down, and Holly knew, with absolute clarity, the moment he regretted it.

His hand let go of hers and raked through his hair. The sound then was one of tense silence.

'We didn't—' he started.

'I *was* there, Daniel,' Holly interrupted. She didn't need to be told that they hadn't used a condom.

He nodded, only it wasn't contraception that was troubling him, it was the closeness, the absolute abandon that he had never felt with another.

He couldn't pretend that they hadn't just crossed the line.

And neither could Holly.

Had he tied a red ribbon around it last night and shouted *Surprise!* well, maybe she could have chalked it down to experience, albeit a new one.

This, though, felt like she had just handed over her soul, only for it to be promptly handed back.

'Are you on the Pill?'

There were many ways this question could be asked, Holly thought. A necessary way, like a doctor. The hopeful way of a lover wanting to pounce.

Or the Daniel way—please, God, tell me you are.

She didn't answer and he got up and sat on the edge of the bed, reaching for his jeans.

'Yes, I'm on the Pill,' she finally said, just to put him out of his obvious misery.

Daniel nodded but said nothing.

And she stopped trying.

It was quite a feat for Holly, but she just stopped trying to pretend that this was okay and didn't even bother to wish him a happy Christmas, she just pulled on her pyjamas and headed out to get ready.

Daniel pulled on his jeans, loathing his own silence.

And just like the last time there were repercussions.

Big ones.

He was staring down the barrel of a future but he couldn't get a clear shot for all the obstacles that were in the way.

Hell, he couldn't even promise to be there for his sister when she needed him to stay.

'I'm ready.'

Holly stood at the door, but of course it wasn't that easy. They'd made quite a mess last night. He threw the remnants of their picnic in the bin and she packed up a few things.

And they were done.

'Do you want this?' He held up the bottle of Scotch and she took it in almost a snatch.

And whereas they should have been lingering in bed and then heading down for breakfast, instead they were signing the guest register to Mrs Barrett's disapproving eyes when Holly had to put down the bottle to pick up the pen!

They drove in strained silence on a now clear motorway.

Holly's earrings had stopped flashing and, from his reaction to the morning's events, all hope for them was gone.

'It's left here,' Holly said, even though his phone told them to take a right. 'It's just a bit quicker.'

The village looked gorgeous and they passed a pretty old pub and she already missed the lazy weekend afternoons the mythical 'us' could have spent there.

Had the closeness between them not completely gone.

Had he had the guts to follow his heart.

'Do you want to come in for breakfast?' Holly offered, even though she knew the answer.

'No.'

'Why?' Holly asked, because she needed to hear it.

Daniel stared out at the sleety street and there were times when you really did have to be cruel to be kind and so he gave Holly her answer. 'Because it would mean something to you. Because in Holly's world when the guy she's just slept with comes to her parents' it means something more.'

And she could say, no, it's just breakfast and my mother would never expect me to let you drop me off and not invite you to come in.

But that would be a lie.

If Daniel came in then so too would hope.

'You're right.'

'I can't play happy families, Holly.'

'You don't even want to try.'

'No.' Because over and over it had failed to work out.

'I'm going to go,' Daniel said, 'and you're going to go in and have a wonderful Christmas with your family.'

He got out of the car and started to unload her bags.

'You're not going to change your mind, are you?'

'No.'

'Are you going to go to your father's?'

'I'll drop off the presents and then I'm going to go home and catch up on some sleep.'

And it hurt that he'd rather get back on the motorway and spend Christmas alone than come in and spend Christmas with her.

'I don't know what to say,' Holly admitted.

She should leave it there really, given him a wave and show what a good detached lover she could be.

That wasn't her, though, and so, just as he climbed back into his car to leave, Holly spoke.

'I don't get you.'

'Holly, let's not do this.'

'No, let's.' Holly's smile was black. 'You see, Daniel, I don't think you're an utter bastard. A bit of one perhaps but if you really thought I was going to go and get stupid ideas about us from sex, you'd never have got into that crinoline bed last night. I think you'd have slept on the floor, or even in the car, rather than hurt me. And I also believe if a quick shag was what you'd wanted this morning, then for my sake you'd have managed to resist.' And then she said it. 'But it wasn't a quick shag.'

'Oh, that's right, we made love.'

He could be as sarcastic and derisive as he chose to be, but, as she'd said this morning, Holly had been there too.

And she could point that out to him, but the war was won and Daniel was the victor.

'I'm done,' Holly said. 'I really am. I've made enough of a fool of myself over you. And I'm not going to say thank you for the lift because the truth is I wish you'd never come out to the car park yesterday.'

'I came out because I didn't want us to end on a row.'

'Do you know what?' Holly retorted. 'It would have been far easier on me if it had.'

She staggered off under the weight of presents and this time she didn't turn around.

Her mother must have been peeking out of the window though because the door opened before she had to work out how to knock.

'Hi, darling, where's your friend?'

'He's not coming in.'

'Oh! But surely—'

'Mum!' Holly said. 'Please.'

If it wasn't Christmas Day she would love to run to her old room fling herself on her bed and cry but, of course, she couldn't.

Instead, she took her bags into the lounge and placed them beside the tree.

And she kept on hoping, so much so that she half expected a knock on the door and for Daniel to say he'd changed his mind, and maybe he'd stay for breakfast.

Instead, with all the bags by the tree, she stood and walked to the window, just in time to see him drive off.

And that was it, Holly knew.

She was never going to see him again.

They were done.

There was no time to process it, though.

Breakfast, as was traditional in the Jacobs family, was birthday cake. Holly blew out her candles and opened her birthday present from her parents and it was a gorgeous pair of earrings.

She took out her cheap Christmas ones that had now

completely stopped flashing and replaced them with her lovely new silver ones.

Then it was champagne with orange juice, though Holly just had orange juice because she was working tonight.

It was smiles and happy all round and Holly joined in, even if she felt as if a part of her had died.

Adam loved his necklace and in turn she loved the travel wallet he had bought, and they traded their gifts with a smile.

Then relatives started to descend and there were parsnips to peel and stuffing to make and then Drunkle Harry and co. arrived.

'I'll take up your coats,' Holly said.

She went up to her old bedroom and took a breath.

'Holly?'

She turned around as her mother came in and saw that she was holding a snowman bag.

'Is everything okay?'

'Of course it is.' Holly smiled her brightest smile but at the last moment it wavered and Holly was appalled with herself when a tear slipped out and she quickly wiped it away.

'Holly?'

She shook her head, because she was simply not able to talk about Daniel without breaking down.

'Is it your friend that wouldn't come in?' Esther checked, and Holly nodded.

'I don't want to talk about it now,' Holly said, and her voice was all shaky. 'I don't want to start crying and ruin Christmas.'

'I seem to remember saying that just over a year ago,' Esther said. 'I sat in the doctor's and I wanted one more perfect Christmas...'

'And we did.'

'Holly, it was awful. Your dad kept slipping out to cry, I burnt the turkey. Harry got so drunk...'

Holly started to laugh. 'It was still a good Christmas.'

'It turned out to be,' Esther agreed.

In the end they'd all had loads to drink and watched a sad film, which had been a good excuse to cry and just relax and stop pretending they were brave.

'You know, I remember when I forgot your birthday...' They just sat there on Holly's old bed and chalked up all the Christmas fails.

'You remembered it that evening,' Holly said. 'And I got a puppy out of it.'

'You did,' Esther sighed. 'Please tell me what's going on, Holly'

And Holly was about to point out that they could do this another time, but then her mum's hand came over hers.

'I know I've been difficult lately,' Esther said. 'But I can still be here for you.'

It had indeed been a long year, one where at times Holly had felt like she'd lost her mum, but it would seem that she was back now.

It was the best gift to have a cuddle from her mum instead of the other way around.

'The guy who gave me the lift home,' Holly said. 'Daniel. I like him a lot, well, I more than like him. I think he feels a bit the same yet he says we're going nowhere. In fact, he's heading overseas...' She gave a pale smile. 'He couldn't make it any clearer that's he's not interested in anything long term but...'

'You still want more.'

'Yes,' Holly said. 'I've never really felt this way before about anyone, not even close.' The one time she had, it hadn't been reciprocated. 'It's probably for the best, we'd never have worked out. I don't think he has a romantic bone in his body and he's not into Christmas. He's hardly even seeing his family, he just wants to go home to bed...' She shook her head as if to clear it. 'I can't believe I've fallen for someone who'd rather sleep his way through Christmas Day than be with his family.' Holly stood, even though her mum still sat there. 'Come on, we'd better go down.'

'You missed a present,' Esther said, and took a box out of the snowman bag.

'From who?' Holly frowned.

'I don't know,' Esther said. 'I was clearing the paper away when I found it. You brought it with you.'

'No.'

It was a silver box covered in fake snow with a silver bow, and it looked terribly like the ones she had seen in the department store. In fact, it looked a lot like the gift she had been considering getting Daniel.

It couldn't be.

Surely?

She looked at the name on the card.

To Holly
  I hope you have the wonderful Christmas that you deserve.
  Secret Santa

Holly tried not to get her hopes up but her hands were shaking as she undid the bow.

It *had* to be from him.

She gasped as she saw a glass ball decorated with her name in silver, and delicate outlines of holly in jewelled green.

What captivated her, though, was the tiny silver envelope inside the glass that had her name on.

'Who's it from?' Esther asked.

'Him.'

'I thought you said he wasn't romantic.'

'He's not.'

'And that he wasn't into Christmas.'

'He isn't.'

Except Daniel had given her the most beautiful, romantic, Christmassy gift in the world.

It was actually the perfect gift, Holly thought as she held it up and the ball spun round, catching the light, but right now it was the letter inside that entranced her.

When would he have put it in her bag? Holly wondered. While they were at the bed and breakfast? But, no, he must have had it before that and then she realised it must have been when they had dragged her parcels in from the car.

When he'd thought she would never see him again.

Oh, it was so much better than a chocolate stocking!

And *so-o-o* much more frustrating!

'I don't see the point,' her father said as Holly hung it on the tree. 'Why would you go to the bother of writing a note that the other person isn't going to read?'

'I'm not sure,' Holly admitted.

'It's like those fire alarms,' mused Drunkle Harry. 'In case of emergency, break the glass.'

'There won't be any emergencies, Uncle Harry.' Holly smiled. 'He probably regrets buying it now. He told me he doesn't want me. I shan't be seeing him again.'

CHAPTER FOURTEEN

HE WAS THE FOOL. Daniel knew it.

As he watched Holly walk to her house in his rear-view mirror, that was exactly how he felt. She was buckling under the weight of presents, and then the door opened and her mother dashed out to help.

He could see her mother's bright silk scarf tied around her head and her slender body and guessed, rightly, it would have been one hell of a year for the family.

And he wanted to go in, to the warmth, to the laughter and fun.

He just didn't know how.

Christmas had always been a let-down.

A huge one.

The build-up would start and it had taken years for him to work out that the promise never came true.

And he was right not to go in, he knew, because it wouldn't be a friend dropping in for Christmas.

Holly was the big one.

The one to whom you promised things like for ever. And those were promises he felt in no position to give, so he started the engine and drove away.

The roads felt empty. Probably because most people were already where they wanted to be.

He pulled into the service station, the one opposite

but identical to the one where they had stopped last night and bought cinnamon and nutmeg coffee and went back to the car and drank it.

Really, Holly had ruined coffee for ever because, though it tasted as bad as it had last night, there was a certain warmth to it, this pleasantness.

He opened the glove box and looked at his gift from Holly, and the ridiculous thing was that he half hoped for a Daniel & Holly snowglobe and some crazy declaration of her love.

He read the card.

To Daniel
From Secret Santa

There wasn't even a kiss!

Well, he guessed there would be something more meaningful inside the wrapping. He opened it slowly and then frowned as a tube of lip balm fell into his palm.

A lip balm?

An expensive lip balm perhaps, but even so…

And then he realised it was Holly's attempt at being bland. Holly doing what he had told her to do and not be so serious about things.

Yet suddenly he was.

He watched as an elderly woman got out of a car and walked towards another. And some children got out and ran to her.

It must be their turn to have granny for Christmas.

Perhaps the families weren't speaking, Daniel pondered, because no one in either car waved to the other.

Yet the kids and the granny were all smiling.

They were somehow making it work.

He thought of Holly, sitting crying, contemplating a

taxi, simply desperate to get home. And he thought of his mother and all the Christmases she'd missed out on.

There were families fighting to be together, longing to be with each other, and there he was, running from his.

He was tired of running.

His phone started to ring; it was Maddie, of course, wanting to know how long it would be till he got there.

'About an hour, I think.'

'Have you got me a present?'

'Maybe.' Daniel smiled.

And then it was a case of please, please, please, could he stay for Christmas dinner.

He was about to say no but then he thought of what Holly had said—that it was embarrassing for Amelia, rather than him.

He could do dinner surely?

'Yes,' he said, and was almost deafened by her squeal. 'I'll see you soon, Maddie. Happy Christmas.'

He loathed that he hadn't been able to make it a happy Christmas for the woman who mattered to him the most.

And so, what was the second-best thing he could do?

He pinched one of Holly's cards from the door pocket and wrote one out for Maddie. Then he drove to his rather odd family and took out the bag that held presents and knocked at the door.

'Daniel!' His father greeted him with a handshake.

Despite the hurts of the past and the hurts of this morning, this Christmas *was* still somehow special. Something had changed in Daniel.

'I love it!' Maddie opened the tiny package and took out a silver neck chain with a little elephant charm with crystal eyes and then she read a certificate that said she'd adopted an elephant. 'Look, Daddy!'

Professor Chandler frowned and put on his glasses

to read the certificate. 'She's adopted an elephant?' He frowned. 'For Christmas?'

He had no idea, Daniel thought.

None.

Yet at least he was trying harder than he had when Daniel had been small because when Maddie whispered in her father's ear, he actually listened and then stood. 'We'll be back in a moment.'

That left Daniel and Amelia and she flushed an unflattering shade of puce and attempted to voice what was on her mind. 'About what happened last year…'

'Nothing happened,' Daniel said. 'And nothing ever shall. Let's just leave it there and focus on Maddie.'

Done.

And he turned as the reason he was here walked into the lounge carrying a very large box that was terribly, and therefore beautifully, wrapped by her.

'I chose this,' Maddie said. 'Jessica said you might not want it as you're travelling but we can keep it here for you when you've gone! You're going to love it.'

Intrigued, Daniel peeled back the wrapper on a very large box and then he gave a very delighted smile, especially at the thought of Jessica trying to dissuade Maddie from her purchase. It was a pink plastic popcorn-maker, with a happy picture of mother and daughter and mountains of popcorn on the box.

'I do love it,' Daniel said, and saw that it even came with a little bag of popping corn.

'You really like it?' Maddie checked, and when Daniel nodded she turned to her father. 'See! I told you.'

'You did indeed,' Professor Chandler agreed. 'Maddie, why don't you get Daniel his other present from under the tree?'

It was a wallet.

A very nice leather one and far from bland it made him smile, given where his had disappeared to last night!

'Thank you.'

And so to dinner.

Amelia declined wine, Daniel noted, and so did he, which he was very glad about given that as Christmas pudding was served his phone rang.

'They'll be wanting me to do a shift,' Daniel said when he saw who it was.

'Tell them fat chance,' his father suggested.

Except he said yes, but only because it was a night shift at The Primary and it was where Holly would be.

Perhaps he could make this a happier Christmas after all.

Or completely spoil it for her?

'I'll need to take food in,' Daniel said, because knowing that lot they would turn it into a party.

'You can take the popcorn machine in.' Maddie smiled.

'I'll see if there's anything nice you can take in,' their father said, and stood.

'Popcorn *is* nice!' Maddie insisted.

'Of course it is,' Marcus said, and he smiled at Daniel over her head. 'So nice that there might not be enough to go around.'

He had mellowed, Daniel realised as he followed his father into a very spacious kitchen, lined with all the mod-cons, all sparkling from lack of use.

Maybe he could, as Holly had suggested, try talking to him.

'There's some pâté and potted...' Marcus said, as he rummaged through the large basket of goodies.

'Dad,' Daniel interrupted. 'I went and saw Maddie perform in her nativity play.'

'I heard that you did. There's probably a ham in the fridge…'

'Dad!' Daniel couldn't give a damn about the ham. 'You should have been there.'

'Oh, come on, Daniel, do you really expect me to cancel surgery because—?'

'Yes,' Daniel said, and then he said it again. 'Yes!' he urged. 'When Maddie's a teenager she might want nothing to do with you but right now she does. You need to be there for the things that matter to her.'

Daniel watched as his father stood there, not cross at the discussion, more confused. 'You've got a secretary.' Daniel thought of Iris. 'I actually looked after one of your old ones the other day. Iris Morrison.'

'She was very efficient.'

'And very under-utilised. She would have loved to factor in your home life. Why don't you go through the calendar and mark out some days for the coming year, like Maddie's birthday and things, and have your secretary organise your schedule around that?'

'I could do that.' Marcus nodded.

He simply accepted the advice and it was then that Daniel realised that sometimes people simply needed to be told. Sometimes the cleverest of people needed help with what others considered the simplest of things.

And so, while they were on the subject, Daniel pushed on. 'And instead of three hours at the club this afternoon, why not take her for ten minutes to the park?'

'She likes the club, there's a playroom there.'

'No, Dad.' Daniel shook his head. 'She hates it.'

'Did you?'

And he could score some points here, Daniel knew,

he could stick the boot in and bring up, oh, so many, many things.

But it was Christmas.

And, more than that, this discussion wasn't about him. It was about a wary-looking little girl who now stood at the kitchen door. 'What are you two talking about?'

Daniel looked at his father, who stared back at his son for a moment and then turned to his daughter. 'I was just saying to your brother that we might go for a walk to the park after dinner if he wanted to come.'

'The park?' Maddie checked. 'The one with swings?'

'Yes.'

'And are you coming?' Maddie asked her brother as Amelia came in.

'I can't,' Daniel said. 'I need to go home and get some sleep and Holly will be back from her family soon...' He shamelessly borrowed Holly, but even if not physically present, by God, it had helped to have her sort of by his side today.

'Holly?' Amelia frowned.

'You met her in the department store the other week.'

'Sounds serious,' his father said, because if it was running into weeks for his son, then it must be.

They had worked at the same hospital after all and word got around!

'It's starting to look that way,' Daniel agreed.

It had actually been starting to look that way for quite some time now but he'd been doing his best not to see what had been right there under his nose.

Yes, try as he might not to be, he was still his father's son.

Though that might not be such a bad thing, Daniel realised, because even a rather old leopard could change its spots.

With a hefty nudge, of course.

As he was about to leave he gave Maddie the card he had written for her in the car.

'What does "ten school pick-ups" mean?' she asked.

'That you've got ten treats next year, though not all in a row.'

'But you're going away.'

'No,' Daniel said. 'I'm not. I might go on holiday, of course, but I'm not leaving you for a whole year...'

And maybe it made no sense to some, she was his half-sister after all, but as her little arms wrapped around his neck, staying close made perfect sense to Daniel.

Maddie was his sister and for her he would be here.

It was a good Christmas.

A great one even, for, as he climbed into the car with his pink plastic popcorn-maker, he watched as his father stood outside, with his daughter hanging off his hand, ready to go to the park.

It was the first time that his father had waved him goodbye.

Ever.

And, because it was Christmas, Daniel tooted and waved back as he drove off.

They looked almost like a normal family!

CHAPTER FIFTEEN

THE MOTORWAY BEHAVED and the drive was made so much easier in her mother's car. Holly had said that she would return it in a couple of days but was seeing in the New Year in London.

With friends and bubbles. She was going to keep all her resolutions this year—one being to be more sophisticated in her love life, and so never make such a fool of herself again with men.

Hell, and if she was ever to have a one-night stand again, she would call the shots—she would climb out of bed, get dressed and walk off without a word. The thought made Holy smirk.

Next year, though.

Right now she knew she had to feel this pain. She had Daniel's present swathed in bubble wrap on the passenger seat and she knew that this year Boxing Day would more like Box of Tissues Day!

Holly got to the hospital and parked, then unloaded all the food her mother had prepared for the night staff. There was rather a lot! She staggered again through the car park and was under the bright lights of the ambulance bay when she heard her name being called.

'Holly!'

A gruff voice had her turn around and she saw a little group standing around a wheelchair.

Holly made her way over, and as she did so a delighted smile split her face. There was Albert, sitting in the wheelchair with a drip attached to a pole and wearing a heavy Christmas jumper and a woolly hat.

She hardly recognised him.

'What are you doing, sitting out here with pneumonia?' Holly both scolded and smiled as she spoke.

'The nurses on the ward said the same,' Albert admitted, 'but it's too stuffy up there.'

'He wanted to come out for some air,' the elder woman explained. 'I'm Dianne, his niece.'

'It's lovely to meet you.'

'This is Emily,' Albert proudly introduced his family. 'She's both my great-niece and god-daughter. They brought me in some Christmas dinner and Emily has made me these.' He opened a tin and showed some beautifully decorated mince pies. 'Take one for your break,' Albert offered.

'I think Holly's got enough food to be going on with,' Dianne said when she saw Holly hesitate.

Usually she didn't accept food from patients and Dianne was right, more mince pies were the very last thing she needed. But, Holly guessed, it must be rather nice for Albert who had spent the last years begging to have food to give some.

'I'll have it on my break,' Holly said. 'If you could just…'

Dianne laughed and selected a pie and added it to the mountain of food that Holly carried.

'I'd better get inside,' she said to the little family. 'Happy Christmas!'

'And to you, Holly.'

'You made it.' Kay beamed as Holly came in. 'And you're early!'

'Someone can go home,' Holly offered, because the staff had done the same for her on the Christmas party night.

'Well, I'll send Anna home. Laura isn't getting here till later so I'm hanging around till then. I have to say, though, for Christmas night it's pretty quiet. Maybe, for once, everyone's behaving.'

Holly had worked a couple and maybe there were jinxing themselves by admitting it, but it actually was quiet. Christmas night was often the busiest with feuding families as well as too much food and alcohol combined. Also there was sometimes the very sick who had held on for that special day.

But, yes, tonight was quiet—at least it was in Emergency, though Kay soon told her that it was otherwise elsewhere.

'Theatre is busy and Maternity is steaming.'

'Who's on tonight?' Holly asked, and they glanced up at the doctors' board and saw that Daniel Chandler was down to work in Emergency tonight.

'We've got…' Kay frowned. 'That can't be right, he's left.'

'No,' Anna called out. 'We had to ring everyone but Daniel agreed to work it.'

And Holly blinked.

She couldn't do this.

She could not keep saying goodbye.

Or, worse than that, she could not keep getting her hopes up because that was what she repeatedly did.

Well, not any more, they were done.

No way would Boxing Day be spent in his bed.

Two-Strikes-and-You're-Out Dr Chandler.

He came in then, carrying boxes and food and with a mince pie on top of it all. Unshaven and gorgeous, he gave her a smile.

'Take your stuff around to the staffroom,' Kay told them, though for Holly it was a rather awkward walk.

'I see you have a mince pie.' Holly said, determined to keep this about the patients rather than them. 'Is that one of Albert's?'

'It is,' Daniel said, and told her he'd been outside chatting with them too. 'The family's moving to the country and apparently there's a little cottage on the grounds. Albert and Dianne both happily admit they'd kill each other under the same roof, but if he has the cottage he can have his privacy and they can keep an eye—'

'He's going to live there?'

'Yep,' Daniel said as they arrived at the staffroom and started to unload all the food. 'Great, isn't it?'

It truly was.

'Why have you brought in a popcorn-maker?' Holly asked.

'Don't you like popcorn?'

'I love popcorn.'

'Then I shall make you some later.'

Holly said nothing, she just headed to the changing room and arrived at the nurses' station a few minutes later in her scrubs and wearng her Christmas earrings.

Everyone was gathered, even Daniel.

'Happy birthday, Holly…' the call went up!

Kay went into her bottomless bag and pulled out a parcel. 'That's from all of us. We were going to do you a cake but…'

'I've had a lot of cake today!'

'We'll do cake next year,' Kay said. 'For your thirtieth.'

Holly groaned. 'Please, don't remind me! Anyway, I'm not working next year, I'm putting in my request now.'

'Did your mother tell you to do that?' Kay asked.

'I shan't be at my mother's on my thirtieth.' Holly smiled sweetly. 'I'll be getting drunk and having anonymous sex with a stranger.'

Kay puffed out her cheeks and tutted but everyone else laughed, even Daniel, and she was proud of herself indeed.

She would get over him.

Holly just had to get through tonight.

She opened her present and found it was a gorgeous jumper that she'd seen online a while ago. She had shown it to Anna, but it hadn't been available in her size.

Yes, she had very good friends.

She read her card and even Nora had taken the time to sign it.

'How's Paul?' Holly asked.

'He's fantastic. He even remembered where he'd hidden Nora's present.' Kay beamed. 'It was in with the lentils.'

'Well, thank God he came out of his coma to remember.'

'It's an eternity ring. No doubt she'll be down later to show it off to all the night staff...' And then her voice trailed off and she looked at Daniel. 'Are you wearing lip gloss?' Kay frowned.

'I am.'

'I can't keep up these days, I have to admit. Men wearing make-up...'

'I like it,' Daniel said. 'It keeps my lips soft, supple and kissable.'

There was something different about him that Holly couldn't put her finger on.

He wasn't at all aloof, he was lighter, funnier and now a part of the team, but it was more than that.

It was as if Daniel had become Daniel.

And, even more so, she wanted him.

CHAPTER SIXTEEN

'HAPPY CHRISTMAS, HOLLY.'

With just an hour left of the big day, and only a couple of patients trickling through, he found her standing at the nurses' station, pulling up some antibiotics that weren't even due yet, and he said what he wished he had said this morning.

Holly was very glad that he hadn't wished her a happy Christmas then, only because she'd have flung it back at him and said he'd ruined it.

Twenty-three hours into Christmas Day she was ready to hear it.

'Thank you.' She smiled. 'And to you.'

It *had* been a happy Christmas, Holly thought as she tapped the little air bubbles out of the syringe.

Despite the tears to come and the hurt yet to heal, it had still somehow managed to be the best Christmas and birthday she'd ever known.

'Was Santa good to you?' he asked.

'He was,' Holly said, wishing he would leave her alone, because it was hard to chat and play friends, but she tried. 'And Secret Santa was *very* good to me.' She looked into those absolute navy eyes, and there was still no silver, no little aqua dots, and she knew she loved him. 'Though he went way over budget...'

'Count yourself lucky. I got a lip balm.'

'The crème de la crème of lip balms,' Holly corrected him.

'Was I to think of you when I applied it?' Daniel asked, and it was he now who looked for a deeper meaning.

'No.' She shook her head. 'It was my I-am-so-over-you present. A bit nicer than I'd have got for others but certainly not in the chocolate stocking category.'

'What's wrong with a chocolate stocking?' Kay asked as she bustled in to get her bag and finally go home.

'Nothing,' Holly said.

In fact, a chocolate stocking was a whole lot less confusing than Daniel, and his romantic gifts and come-to-bed eyes, followed by the silent treatment the morning after.

Aaggh!

She wanted to scream but she didn't and no way, *no way* would she ask what was in the letter.

'Did you get any presents, Daniel?' Kay asked.

'I got a wallet from my father and stepmother,' Daniel said, 'and a popcorn-maker from my sister. We had a good day.'

'You stayed for dinner?' Holly frowned.

'I did.'

'Don't you get on?' Kay asked.

'Not really,' Daniel said. 'Though it's my stepmum that's the problem at the moment. Still, I do have a young sister...'

'How old is she?'

'Five,' Daniel said.

'And so how old is your stepmother?' Kay exclaimed in her less-than-tactful way.

'Twenty-seven.'

'Dear God!' Kay was stunned. 'That would be hard.'

'Actually,' Daniel said, picking up a file for the next patient, 'it's not. Much to Amelia's disappointment.'

Holly and Kay looked at each other as Daniel went to walk off. Holly could not believe he was finally being open about it, and as for Kay...

No, she wasn't subtle and she was also very, very shrewd.

'Did she come on to you, Daniel?'

Holly held her breath, wondering what his reaction would be.

'Last year.' Daniel nodded.

'And did you respond in kind?'

'Kay!' Holly admonished. Kay just went too far at times and Daniel clearly agreed because he turned around.

'No, I did not!' Daniel was all snobby and angry but it would seem Kay wasn't being nosey, she was just being very, very honest.

'I did!' She went purple in the face. 'Why do you think I work every Christmas? I'm trying to keep away from Eamon's twin?'

She was Irish, she was funny and it *was* Christmas night.

'One year his fecking mother made the same jumper and gave it to them for Christmas and so they were both wearing it...'

Holly watched a smile inch over Daniel's face as Kay proceeded to tell her story in the way only the Irish could.

'Well, I had everyone at the Christmas table, they were all getting on with their starters, and, given I had to get things ready, I ate mine quickly. I went into the kitchen to sort out the main course. I was taking the foil off the turkey and then Eamon came up behind me and he pinched my bottom and then we had a kiss, as you do...'

'Indeed,' Daniel said.

'It was quite a kiss actually,' Kay elaborated, 'but I told him that I needed to get on with dinner and that I'd deal with him better later and I gave it a little squeeze...'

And Holly laughed as Daniel's eyes popped a little.

'Then I walked through with the turkey and there was Eamon, sitting where I'd left him, and his brother was walking behind me... I knew I'd just got off with my husband's twin.'

They laughed so much!

Just laughed and laughed because somehow all families had their dramas and tales, all families were a little crazy.

Especially at Christmas.

'Did you tell Eamon?' Holly asked, when she had remembered how to breathe.

'Of course not,' Kay said. 'I mean...' She stopped talking in mid-sentence and looked over Holly's shoulder, and Kay's expression was so stunned that both Daniel and Holly turned around to see what had halted Kay in her tracks. 'Louise!'

It was Kay's daughter, accompanied by a very nervous-looking young man whose arm she was clinging onto.

'I was going to call you from Maternity...' Louise started to explain to her mother and then stopped as clearly another contraction hit. 'I don't think I'm going to get there.'

And Kay, the most competent, the most experienced, the utter glue of the department and, Holly guessed, her family too, just stood there not moving, like a tree in the middle of a field.

'Come on, Holly.' It was Daniel who moved.

He went over, shook the man's hand and found out his name—Gilbert—and then he guided Louise into a cubicle and Holly followed them all in. 'Let's help you up onto the trolley...' Daniel started, but Louise held onto the metal edges for dear life and started to bear down.

'Why don't we let the maternity department know?' Daniel suggested.

'I just have,' Kay said. She was present now, though not fully recovered from the shock of her daughter's arrival, but her voice was very deliberately steady and calm. 'They'll send someone just as soon as they're able to.'

Kay had brought in a delivery pack and Holly and Daniel were getting Louise up onto the gurney as she spoke on. 'They're very busy up there and, given we've got a registrar and,' she added, 'I'm also a midwife...'

'We'll be fine,' Daniel said in his composed, deep voice just as he had the night Paul had come in.

And he was calm, though not so aloof now, for he gave Kay's shoulder a little squeeze.

It was everything that was needed now.

CHAPTER SEVENTEEN

'WE'LL BE MORE than fine,' Kay said as she rallied. 'Now, Louise—' she was as direct as ever '—do you want me to wait outside? Just say if it's awkward for you to have your mother here.'

'No-o-o-o!' Louise shouted as another contraction took over and she clutched both her mother and her partner's arms and bore down.

Holly was very quickly opening up the delivery pack.

This baby really was in a hurry to be born!

'When did the contractions start?' Holly asked.

'Only an hour or so ago,' Gilbert answered. 'Though she's felt a bit off all day.'

'Why didn't you say when I called?' Kay asked.

'She didn't want you to worry, given how busy it is at Christmas,' Gilbert said, 'and we thought it would take ages.' He was trying to take in the speed of it all.

So was Holly—the head was almost out.

'Louise,' Daniel said. 'A big push, please.'

He was very polite as he made his request and Louise went from red to purple as she complied and then she made a request of her own. 'Can my mum deliver my baby?' she asked.

'I think that would be rather wonderful,' Daniel agreed.

When Kay came round, Holly watched as Daniel gave Kay's shoulder not one squeeze but two.

The first was to say, *I'm here beside you*, because for Kay this was the most important delivery of her life.

The second squeeze told her that she'd got this all under control—a midwife, a mother, a fabulous nurse, Kay was about to deliver her own grandchild.

And she coached her daughter well and soon a little head with dark hair was out and, with this push, the baby would be here.

'Oh...' Kay guided her grandbaby out into the world and delivered the vigorous bundle up onto Louise's stomach.

Daniel was there so he could step in if Kay became overwhelmed but it was simply a very beautiful birth.

'A girl,' Louise cried. 'Gilbert, we've got a little girl!'

He was a very proud father and Daniel handed Gilbert the scissors so he could cut the cord as the tiny little girl started to cry.

Holly was close to tears herself.

All births were beautiful but this one felt especially so.

And yet Holly felt sad.

'You have a visitor...' Laura popped her head around the curtain.

Eamon was there to take his wife home and when Louise called for him to come and meet his granddaughter he got the surprise of his life.

Holly knew she couldn't hold it together any more and when the midwife arrived from Maternity she slipped out and went and hid in the dark small theatre to let a few tears trickle out.

She had never felt so happy and sad at the same time.

She not only loved him, she really *liked* Daniel too,

and she didn't want him to be gone. She didn't *want* to have to get over him!

So she sat and decided to have a little Holly pity party and for ten minutes she sat there, but just as she was going to sneak out to sort out her face she heard his voice.

'Holly?'

She was too tired to even jump.

He didn't turn on the lights and she didn't turn her face to where he stood at the door.

'You have a namesake—they're going to call the baby Holly.'

'That's nice.'

'You forgot to do something today and so did I.'

He turned on the big bright lights then and he politely ignored that her mascara was down to her chin as he held up two Advent calendars.

'There's still five minutes left of Christmas.'

Even chocolate couldn't help with the way she felt, but Holly gave a thin smile and took her calendar and went to open the double doors.

'What do you think it might be?' Daniel asked, but Holly didn't answer. It was the last chocolate, the last special day, the last of them.

'A chocolate-covered gold leaf star?' he suggested. 'Or a little white chocolate dove filled...'

Oh, dear, just as he was getting the hang of Christmas the master chocolatier failed him. It was another little ball with red and green sticking out and a dusting of icing sugar.

'I think this must be why they ended up in the discount store,' Holly said.

They had come this far with their Advent calendars and so were sort of duty bound to eat them really. Even as they opened their mouths and dropped the chocolates in, both hoped they were wrong and that this time it would taste delicious.

It didn't.

'I hate glacé cherries.' Holly pulled a face and swallowed the bitter chocolate.

'And me,' Daniel said as he did the same. 'I think the chocolate's burnt!'

Then they looked at each other and, though she smiled, it was a sad one.

He loathed that he had hurt her.

Really hurt her, he knew, because they *had* made love this morning, and he had been an utter bastard afterwards.

'Don't you want to know what's in the letter?' Daniel asked.

'I'm going to smash it in the morning and find out,' Holly said, and they both smiled at the vision of her angrily taking a hammer to that blasted ball.

But then she started to cry.

'Go away,' she said.

'I can't,' Daniel said. 'Holly, I've been trying to leave for weeks but I can't. You've got me working Christmas, and adopting elephants and lining up in department stores for three hours just to get the perfect gift.'

'Three hours?'

'Which was plenty of time to change my mind, but I didn't,' Daniel said. 'I'm even arguing with elves...'

'Why were you arguing with elves?'

'I don't think my letter was effusive enough for them and, please, when you smash the decoration, bear in mind—'

'We both know I'm not going to smash it.' Holly sighed, but then she frowned. 'Bear in mind what?'

'That it was written before we…' He really struggled with the next two words. 'Made love.'

She smiled at her small victory.

'I shall bear it in mind!' Holly agreed. 'So what does it say?'

'I can't tell you. Elf rules.'

Holly rolled her eyes.

'Actually, if you guess correctly, I'll tell you so.'

'I don't want to guess.'

'What do you *think* the note might say?' Daniel insisted.

And so Holly thought for a moment and she smiled before delivering another little victory. 'I think it says "Are you on the Pill?"'

Daniel also smiled at her vindictive reference to that morning. 'I'm going to love rowing with you.'

And she could have sworn her earrings flashed, or was it hope that darted past her heart as he made reference to a future *us*.

Stop it, she told herself.

'What would you *like* the letter to say?' Daniel pushed.

And she knew what she'd like it to say, but she diluted it down, of course. 'That you like me a lot.'

'Correct,' Daniel said in sarcastic response. 'I got the little elves to write, "Dear Holly, I like you a lot." What would you *really* like it to say?'

'Don't,' Holly said, 'because I'll get all carried away and then…'

'You can get carried away, Holly. What would you like the letter to say?'

And she would be sophisticated next year.

'That you love me?' She said it as a question but it was the truth—it was what she wanted the letter to say.

She had no pride left and the emotional desert that was Daniel would just have to deal with it.

He gave a small snort at her soppy response. 'We've slept together twice, Holly.'

'I know.' She worried her bottom lip. 'It's embarrassing really...'

'What is? Your devotion to me?'

Holly nodded.

'I like it.' He grinned. 'Next guess?'

'No.' She shook her head. 'I don't like this game.'

His mouth gaped open and for the second time in their short history he pointed at her. Caught! 'You wanted it to say "Marry me"!'

'No, I didn't.'

'Holly, I don't hold out much hope for us if we're already reduced to lying. Did you or did you not hope it said that?'

'In very abstract wild dreams, possibly, while knowing of course it didn't say that...'

She had to know what it said.

'I'm going to go out to the car now and smash it!'

She was.

Holly was through being led down some emotional garden path by Daniel.

It was four minutes to midnight and with any luck that stupid ball would be history soon.

'Holly.' Daniel caught her arm as she went to go. 'Perhaps I should tell you that, for an inordinate sum, you can purchase a duplicate letter.'

'Oh.'

He opened his new wallet and instead of a condom nestled in the corner there was another shiny silver package and in the teeniest letters she saw her name.

It was rather tricky to open, but finally Holly got the letter out and she stared at the tiny squiggles.

'I can't read it.'

This was torture!

He went into a drawer and took out the magnifying glasses used for the most delicate suturing and she put them on and the tiny words came into clear view.

Dearest Holly,

I can only say this from a distance and only once I'm safely gone.

Sorry for being so contrary. You truly didn't deserve it. I want you to know that I've been cold and held back because, in truth, if I ever was going to settle down, and if there ever was that one person, then it would be you.

Daniel xxx

'The elf didn't approve,' Daniel said.

'Well, I do.'

As he took the magnifying glasses off her a part of her didn't want him to, she just wanted to stare at his words. But as the world came back to normal size she stared instead at him.

Into those absolute navy eyes that she had fallen in love with on sight.

And now she could admit it, not just to herself but to him.

'I love you.'

She'd never said it before, well, to her family and the dog and things, but not in the way she said it now.

'I know,' Daniel said. 'And I can't believe that I didn't want you to. I can't believe that I kept trying to avoid hearing those words. But *you're* the reason I couldn't leave and the reason I want to stay...'

Oh, there was work, and there was his sister, but his world had only fallen into place when she had entered it.

Life had started to get better the day Holly had arrived and it had made him not want to leave.

'It's you,' Daniel told her. 'And if you'll have me, and we hurry, you might get that winter wedding.'

'You mean it?'

'I more than mean it,' Daniel said. 'I've even chosen the location. We're getting married in a castle.'

Later he would tell her about a family holiday and happy memories and miniature castles and motorways on Christmas mornings and all of those things, but right now there was but one thing to be said.

'I love you, Holly.'

He said the words that he never had to any other and then he lowered his mouth to hers.

It was a soft and delicious kiss and it tasted of glacé cherries with a faint trace of bitter, burnt chocolate.

And it was wonderful.

* * * * *

If you enjoyed this story, check out these other great reads from Carol Marinelli

SEDUCED BY THE SHEIKH SURGEON
SEDUCED BY THE HEART SURGEON

THE SHEIKH'S BABY SCANDAL
DI SIONE'S INNOCENT CONQUEST

All available now!

MILLS & BOON®
Hardback – December 2016

ROMANCE

A Di Sione for the Greek's Pleasure	Kate Hewitt
The Prince's Pregnant Mistress	Maisey Yates
The Greek's Christmas Bride	Lynne Graham
The Guardian's Virgin Ward	Caitlin Crews
A Royal Vow of Convenience	Sharon Kendrick
The Desert King's Secret Heir	Annie West
Married for the Sheikh's Duty	Tara Pammi
Surrendering to the Vengeful Italian	Angela Bissell
Winter Wedding for the Prince	Barbara Wallace
Christmas in the Boss's Castle	Scarlet Wilson
Her Festive Doorstep Baby	Kate Hardy
Holiday with the Mystery Italian	Ellie Darkins
White Christmas for the Single Mum	Susanne Hampton
A Royal Baby for Christmas	Scarlet Wilson
Playboy on Her Christmas List	Carol Marinelli
The Army Doc's Baby Bombshell	Sue MacKay
The Doctor's Sleigh Bell Proposal	Susan Carlisle
The Baby Proposal	Andrea Laurence
Maid Under the Mistletoe	Maureen Child

MILLS & BOON®
Large Print – December 2016

ROMANCE

The Di Sione Secret Baby	Maya Blake
Carides's Forgotten Wife	Maisey Yates
The Playboy's Ruthless Pursuit	Miranda Lee
His Mistress for a Week	Melanie Milburne
Crowned for the Prince's Heir	Sharon Kendrick
In the Sheikh's Service	Susan Stephens
Marrying Her Royal Enemy	Jennifer Hayward
An Unlikely Bride for the Billionaire	Michelle Douglas
Falling for the Secret Millionaire	Kate Hardy
The Forbidden Prince	Alison Roberts
The Best Man's Guarded Heart	Katrina Cudmore

HISTORICAL

Sheikh's Mail-Order Bride	Marguerite Kaye
Miss Marianne's Disgrace	Georgie Lee
Her Enemy at the Altar	Virginia Heath
Enslaved by the Desert Trader	Greta Gilbert
Royalist on the Run	Helen Dickson

MEDICAL

The Prince and the Midwife	Robin Gianna
His Pregnant Sleeping Beauty	Lynne Marshall
One Night, Twin Consequences	Annie O'Neil
Twin Surprise for the Single Doc	Susanne Hampton
The Doctor's Forbidden Fling	Karin Baine
The Army Doc's Secret Wife	Charlotte Hawkes

MILLS & BOON®
Hardback – January 2017

ROMANCE

A Deal for the Di Sione Ring	Jennifer Hayward
The Italian's Pregnant Virgin	Maisey Yates
A Dangerous Taste of Passion	Anne Mather
Bought to Carry His Heir	Jane Porter
Married for the Greek's Convenience	Michelle Smart
Bound by His Desert Diamond	Andie Brock
A Child Claimed by Gold	Rachael Thomas
Defying Her Billionaire Protector	Angela Bissell
Her New Year Baby Secret	Jessica Gilmore
Slow Dance with the Best Man	Sophie Pembroke
The Prince's Convenient Proposal	Barbara Hannay
The Tycoon's Reluctant Cinderella	Therese Beharrie
Falling for Her Wounded Hero	Marion Lennox
The Surgeon's Baby Surprise	Charlotte Hawkes
Santiago's Convenient Fiancée	Annie O'Neil
Alejandro's Sexy Secret	Amy Ruttan
The Doctor's Diamond Proposal	Annie Claydon
Weekend with the Best Man	Leah Martyn
One Baby, Two Secrets	Barbara Dunlop
The Tycoon's Secret Child	Maureen Child

MILLS & BOON®
Large Print – January 2017

ROMANCE

To Blackmail a Di Sione	Rachael Thomas
A Ring for Vincenzo's Heir	Jennie Lucas
Demetriou Demands His Child	Kate Hewitt
Trapped by Vialli's Vows	Chantelle Shaw
The Sheikh's Baby Scandal	Carol Marinelli
Defying the Billionaire's Command	Michelle Conder
The Secret Beneath the Veil	Dani Collins
Stepping into the Prince's World	Marion Lennox
Unveiling the Bridesmaid	Jessica Gilmore
The CEO's Surprise Family	Teresa Carpenter
The Billionaire from Her Past	Leah Ashton

HISTORICAL

Stolen Encounters with the Duchess	Julia Justiss
The Cinderella Governess	Georgie Lee
The Reluctant Viscount	Lara Temple
Taming the Tempestuous Tudor	Juliet Landon
Silk, Swords and Surrender	Jeannie Lin

MEDICAL

Taming Hollywood's Ultimate Playboy	Amalie Berlin
Winning Back His Doctor Bride	Tina Beckett
White Wedding for a Southern Belle	Susan Carlisle
Wedding Date with the Army Doc	Lynne Marshall
Capturing the Single Dad's Heart	Kate Hardy
Doctor, Mummy... Wife?	Dianne Drake

MILLS & BOON®

Why shop at millsandboon.co.uk?

Each year, thousands of romance readers find their perfect read at millsandboon.co.uk. That's because we're passionate about bringing you the very best romantic fiction. Here are some of the advantages of shopping at www.millsandboon.co.uk:

* **Get new books first**—you'll be able to buy your favourite books one month before they hit the shops

* **Get exclusive discounts**—you'll also be able to buy our specially created monthly collections, with up to 50% off the RRP

* **Find your favourite authors**—latest news, interviews and new releases for all your favourite authors and series on our website, plus ideas for what to try next

* **Join in**—once you've bought your favourite books, don't forget to register with us to rate, review and join in the discussions

Visit **www.millsandboon.co.uk**
for all this and more today!